His first thought was that she'd been abducted.

Then he realized that the door to her bedroom was open.

He walked past the message written in bold letters in bloodred lipstick: This Is What Happens To Meddlers.

He was relieved to see Bren staring wordlessly at her dresser. He holstered his gun and went to her, wrapping his arms around her waist, drawing her back against him.

"Are you okay, baby?"

She swallowed, then nodded, still too overcome to speak.

"I can't believe I called you. I have a brother in the security business. Another who has more connections in Washington than the president. Yet I called you."

He touched a hand to her shoulder. "You called me because you know in your heart I'd never let anything happen to you."

Dear Reader,

They say that March comes in like a lion, and we've got six fabulous books to help you start this month off with a bang. Ruth Langan's popular series, THE LASSITER LAW, continues with *Banning's Woman*. This time it's the Banning sister, a freshman congresswoman, whose life is in danger. And to the rescue... handsome police officer Christopher Banning, who's vowed to get Mary Bren out of a stalker's clutches—and *into* his arms.

ROMANCING THE CROWN continues with Marie Ferrarella's *The Disenchanted Duke,* in which a handsome private investigator—with a strangely royal bearing—engages in a spirited battle with a beautiful bounty hunter to locate the missing crown prince. And in Linda Winstead Jones's *Capturing Cleo,* a wary detective investigating a murder decides to close in on the prime suspect—the dead man's sultry and seductive ex-wife—by pursuing her romantically. Only problem is, where does the investigation end and romance begin? Beverly Bird continues our LONE STAR COUNTRY CLUB series with *In the Line of Fire,* in which a policewoman investigating the country club explosion must team up with an ex-mobster who makes her pulse race in more ways than one. You won't want to miss RaeAnne Thayne's second book in her OUTLAW HARTES miniseries, *Taming Jesse James,* in which reformed bad-boy-turned-sheriff Jesse James Harte puts his life—not to mention his heart—on the line for lovely schoolteacher Sarah MacKenzie. And finally, in *Keeping Caroline* by Vickie Taylor, a tragedy pushes a man back toward the wife he'd left behind—and the child he never knew he had.

Enjoy all of them! And don't forget to come back next month when the excitement continues in Silhouette Intimate Moments.

Yours,

Leslie J. Wainger
Executive Senior Editor

Please address questions and book requests to:
Silhouette Reader Service
U.S.: 3010 Walden Ave., P.O. Box 1325, Buffalo, NY 14269
Canadian: P.O. Box 609, Fort Erie, Ont. L2A 5X3

Banning's
Woman
RUTH
LANGAN

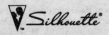

INTIMATE MOMENTS™

Published by Silhouette Books

America's Publisher of Contemporary Romance

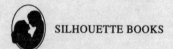

SILHOUETTE BOOKS

ISBN 0-373-27205-7

BANNING'S WOMAN

Books by Ruth Langan

RUTH LANGAN

is an award-winning and bestselling author. Her books have been finalists for the Romance Writers of America RITA Award. Over the years, she has given dozens of print, radio and TV interviews, including *Good Morning America* and *CNN News,* and has been quoted in such diverse publications as *The Wall Street Journal, Cosmopolitan* and *The Detroit Free Press.* Married to her childhood sweetheart, she has raised five children and lives in Michigan, the state where she was born and raised.

For beautiful little Gabrielle Rose,
shiny new link in our chain of love.
And for her parents, Patrick and Randi,
and her sweet brother and sister, Patrick and Nicole.

And as always, for Tom, pure gold.

Prologue

Chevy Chase, Maryland, 1981

Kieran Lassiter nursed his beer and wondered how he would survive the weight of the grief that pressed against his heart. Earlier today, when the casket bearing the body of his son Riordan had been lowered into the ground, it had taken all his courage to remain standing. He'd wanted to sink to his knees and wail like a banshee. To throw himself into the grave and beg to be buried alive. It wasn't the way of things, for a man to bury his son. It should

have been the other way around. He'd had a
full, rich life, married to the same fine woman
for thirty-seven years. He'd been blessed with
a son who'd done his father proud by following him into service as a much-decorated police officer in the city of Washington, D.C.
What's more, Riordan and his wife, Kate, had
given Kieran four lively grandchildren. With
his wife already gone, Kieran was ready to die.
Instead, life had dealt him a cruel blow, and
had taken his son in the prime of his life. It
left him devastated. And feeling suddenly old
and useless.

Giving in to the grief, he allowed the tears
to flow until he was drowning in misery. What
was he to do now? How was he expected to
go on, with his only son torn from his arms?
He didn't want to be here, hiding out like a
frightened old man in his daughter-in-law's
home. In fact, he didn't want to be anywhere
in this world. If the Almighty were merciful,
he would be taken this very night, in order to
be spared the pain of facing another morning.

He heard the creak of the stairs and put on
the fiercest look he could manage, to hide the
tears. "Who's there?"

A small figure stepped out of the shadows. "It's me, Pop. Bren."

"Mary Brendan." The sight of this wee lass always touched a chord in him. When she'd been born, Riordan refused to change the name he'd already picked out for this third child, in anticipation of another son. And so Brendan, which had been the name of Kieran's beloved father, had become Mary Brendan, though everyone in the family shortened it to Bren.

She was tiny, appearing to be no more than six, though she was already eight years old and smart as a whip. Her proud father had often remarked that she was an odd little duck. An old soul, wise beyond her years, who seemed touched with some sort of special powers. It was she who could mend a cut knee or a bloody nose with her gentle care. She who could put a smile on even the saddest face. But this was no fragile hothouse flower. She'd developed an outer toughness in order to survive the daily combat of three brothers.

She may have inherited her mother's fiery hair and her father's unusual blue-green eyes, but her mind was delightfully original.

"What's wrong, lass?"

"I—" her lip quivered "—can't sleep yet."

"I know the feeling." He beckoned her closer and lifted her onto his lap. "Come sit with your old pop for a while. We'll keep each other company."

She snuggled close, aware that he smelled vaguely like her father. "Sister Elizabethine said we should be proud, because Dad was a hero."

"That he was. He gave his life for his partner." Kieran took another blow to the heart and wondered if he could bear the pain. "Greater love hath no man…"

"When I grow up, I'm going to spend my life doing good for other people, too."

"And how do you intend to do that, lass? Will you be a police officer like your father and me?"

She shook her head, sending red curls dancing. "I'm going to find some other way to help people. Dad said if I read enough books and study the lives of heroes, I'll find out what I'm meant to do. I just know I want to do something good." She gave a long, deep sigh. "Pop, I know Dad's gone to heaven, but he hasn't really left. He's still here with us, watching over us."

Kieran wrapped his big arms around her and pressed his face to her hair, struggling to find the words that would bring comfort to them both. "We all want to believe your dad is still here with us."

She looked up. "You, too?"

"Yeah." He drew in a deep breath. "Of course, we can't always have what we want. Life doesn't always go the way we planned it. But your grandmother, God rest her soul, used to say that whenever one door is closed, another opens."

She looked up eagerly. "But Dad doesn't need a door now. He's always here. We just can't always see him."

"That's a nice thought, lass." He saw her eyes fill with tears. "Now what's wrong?"

"Mom's in Cameron's room, reading a bedtime story to him. Dad told me I'd have to be patient because Cameron's the youngest, and he needs Mom more than me."

"Your dad told you that, did he? And when did the two of you have this conversation?"

"Just now. Up in my room."

He drew back to give her a long, slow look. "You know it's wrong to fib, Mary Brendan."

"I know." When she realized what he was

suggesting, her eyes rounded. "Dad was there, Pop. He sat next to me on my bed and told me he'd always be here to watch out for us. He said Donovan would need the most care, because he's so much like you. And he said you would need all of us to fill the hole in your heart. Do you have a hole in your heart, Pop?"

He nodded, suddenly too overcome to speak.

"Dad said you'd tuck me in bed, now that he can't be here to do it." She stared up into his eyes. "Will you? Tuck me in bed?"

Shaken, he got to his feet, cradling her against his chest. "I will, Mary Brendan."

He climbed the stairs and carried her to her room. After settling her under the covers he bent down to brush a kiss over her cheek and tasted the salt. "What's this now? More tears?"

She sniffed. "I'm glad you tucked me in tonight, Pop. But when you go back home, who'll tuck me in then?"

He didn't know where the words came from. Without giving it a moment's thought he said, "Then, I guess I'll just have to stay."

"You mean it? Forever?"

He nodded. "I give you my word, lass. I'll stay here for as long as I'm needed. And if you like, I'll tuck you in every night until you're all grown-up and don't want me around anymore."

"Oh, Pop. Thank you." She wrapped her arms around his neck and hugged him fiercely. "But there'll never be a time when I won't want you around."

In that moment he felt as though the tight band around his heart loosened just a bit.

As he stepped from her room and returned to his chair by the fire, he felt a sense of deep gratitude. That strange, perceptive little girl, who could be so wise or so heartbreakingly tender, had just given him a reason to go on living.

Chapter 1

"Hi, Pop." Cameron Lassiter came breezing through the back door, his attaché case in hand. "Something smells wonderful."

His grandfather, Kieran, took a moment to taste before setting aside the spoon and looking up. "Pea soup. The best I've ever made."

Kieran had remained at his daughter-in-law's home for all these years, cooking, cleaning and helping raise her four children, who were now adults with lives of their own. Still he remained, running the house while Kate, who had returned to law school after the death of her husband, now worked as a family advocate in the poorest section of Washington, D.C.

Just then Kate Lassiter hurried inside, trailed by her son Micah and his wife, Pru, who lived down the street.

"I see it's just another quiet night," Cameron remarked dryly. He turned to greet the rest of his family before tossing aside his jacket and briefcase. "Pop made soup."

"Great. It's blustery out there today." Micah nodded toward the backyard where fiery autumn leaves were engaged in a lively dance.

Cameron had a thought. "Did you bake some bread to go with that soup, Pop?

In reply Kieran picked up a knife and began cutting thick slices of bread on a cutting board. In his best Irish brogue he asked, "You mean you intend to grace us with your presence at supper tonight?"

Cameron grinned. "Yeah. I had plans but they got...changed at the last minute."

Micah picked up on that immediately. "Meaning the latest bimbo dumped you."

"Bimbo? Listen, bro..." Cameron gave Micah a shove hard enough to rattle his bones and send him back against the trestle table.

In turn Micah clapped a big hand on his

younger brother's shoulder. The look in his eye signaled an all-out fight.

Kieran nodded toward the back door. "Out to the yard, the two of you. There's still time to shoot hoops before supper."

Micah lifted his hands in a symbol of defeat. "No need, Pop. We'll behave. At least for now."

"Not good enough. You heard what I—"

Suddenly Pru's voice could be heard from the other room. "Oh, my goodness. Look at this. It's our Bren. On the six-o'clock news."

Everyone went trooping into the great room to stare at the television. When Bren's face came on the screen, they went deadly quiet as the news anchor's voice said, "After an unarmed man was gunned down by a police officer right here in the district, Representative Mary Brendan Lassiter was asked by her party to form a commission to investigate not only this crime, but a string of deaths involving the excessive use of force by police."

At that, Kieran gave a snort of disgust, but quickly quieted as Bren was shown facing a barrage of microphones and reporters, all shouting questions.

A pretty blond reporter called, "Congresswoman, do you support those who say the police have been given too much authority over the lives of ordinary citizens?''

Bren managed a smile. ''I haven't heard it put quite that way. Our committee has found some abuse of power in some select police forces. But that is certainly not the norm. For the most part we find the police to be dedicated professionals who take their jobs very seriously.''

Kieran nodded. ''You tell 'em, lass.''

''Congresswoman Lassiter.'' An earnest young reporter shouted above the din. ''We've heard that police boards across the country have unanimously condemned the wording of the bill your committee is considering. A bill that would encourage the investigation of corruption by an agency independent of the police board. The chief complaint is, of course, that your bill would block the police from investigating their own and weaken the power of the Department of Internal Affairs.''

Bren's smile remained in place. ''I don't see how anyone could speak against a bill that hasn't even been finalized yet. Our committee members are still discussing the language.''

''But you won't deny that such a bill has

been drafted and is being seriously considered?''

Bren chose her words carefully. ''We all realize that if even one innocent person is the
victim of police violence, that is one person
too many. If the police can't monitor their
own, perhaps an outside agency should be
called in. This bill is just one of many solu-
tions our committee is considering.''

''Aren't you also considering setting limits
on the numbers and types of weapons a police
officer may carry?''

''As I said, we are considering many issues.
At this time nothing is written in stone.''

The camera cut away from Bren to the face
of the news anchor in the TV studio who said,
''And so the battle lines are already being
drawn between police officers across America
and the House of Representatives, with freshman Congresswoman Mary Brendan Lassiter
leading the charge.''

''What rubbish.'' Kate Lassiter clicked off
the set and turned to see her sons and father-
in-law looking glum. ''I hope you aren't going
to believe such nonsense before you even get
a chance to talk to Bren.''

"She didn't deny it." Micah's eyes were cold as ice.

"What's worse, she actually admitted it." Kieran pounded a fist into his hand. "How could a Lassiter even consider such a thing as tying the hands of the very ones dedicated to protecting us? Why, it goes against everything the Lassiters have always stood for."

Kate touched a hand to the old man's arm. "You're jumping to conclusions."

"Am I?" Kieran rounded on her, his eyes dark with fury. "Nobody in Congress knows better than our Bren about the dangers a police officer faces every day of his life. That she would even consider for a single moment limiting the use of defensive weapons makes me sick. To say nothing of inviting outsiders to investigate police internal affairs. Who better than the department to clean up its own mess?"

When the phone rang Cameron snatched it up. "Hello. Yeah, we saw her." In an aside to the others he said, "Donovan. He and Andi just saw the news." He listened to the voice on the phone before giving a terse grunt. "That's about the consensus here, too." He paused. "Well now, Donovan, I wouldn't go so far as to say she's a turncoat. But it does sound like our sister has some explaining to do.''

He hung up the phone, then snatched it up when it rang yet again. ''Hello.'' His lips thinned. ''Hey, Bren. We caught your dog-and-pony act on TV. What are you and your committee planning for an encore? Taking books away from teachers?''

He listened, his smile fading, then nodded and said, ''Okay. I'll tell them.''

Kieran stared glumly at the phone. ''I wanted to have a word with her.''

''She was on the run, calling from her cell phone. She said she has to return to her committee meeting. It'll probably run late into the night. She'll try to stop by tomorrow.''

Kieran turned toward the stairs. ''The soup and homemade bread are ready. And there's a Maurice salad in the fridge.''

Micah called after him, ''What about you, Pop? Where are you going?''

''Upstairs to my room. I've lost my appetite.''

''Kieran.'' Kate looped her arm through his, forcing him to turn around. ''Come on, now. We'll eat together.''

The others followed them to the kitchen, where they gathered around the big trestle table. Their mood was subdued as they joined hands.

Kieran's voice rang out. "Bless this food and those gathered here. Bless also those who can't be with us this night, especially our own Mary Brendan, who needs guidance from above. And bless Riordan, who watches over us all. Perhaps he'll give her a nudge in the right direction."

When the blessing was concluded, Micah gave voice to all their thoughts. "I know Bren has to make a lot of compromises in her work in Congress. But I refuse to believe she'd set restrictions on this nation's police forces."

Kate nodded. "I agree. I intend to reserve judgment until I read the words of the bill for myself."

Cameron buttered a slice of bread and tucked into a bowl of steaming soup. "Yeah, but you're her mother. We're her family. I don't think the rest of the country is going to be as willing to wait. That little sixty-second sound byte on the news is the only thing most people will remember. They've already decided that Congresswoman Mary Brendan

Lassiter is tying the hands of the police and making it even easier on the criminals.''

Around the table heads nodded as they realized the difficult position Bren was in. She would have to do some fancy talking to overcome such negative publicity.

"I'm leaving." Juana Sanchez poked her head in the door of Bren's office.

Tall and pretty, her dark hair smoothed into a neat knot at her nape, she'd been the first staff member hired after Bren had been elected to the House of Representatives from Maryland. Juana's first introduction to the Lassiter family had come through Kate, when Juana had been struggling to keep her family together after the death of her young husband. The two women had bonded, and it had been Kate Lassiter who had gently nudged Juana toward finishing high school and then college. Now, fifteen years later, she would soon have her law degree. In the meantime she was the hardest working member of Bren's congressional staff.

"Thanks for staying on, Juana. I'll be leaving soon myself." Bren indicated the stack of documents in front of her.

"From the looks of that, you'll be here all night." Juana couldn't resist sounding like a mother. "Did you take time to eat anything at all today?"

"I had some fruit." Bren saw the quick frown and laughed. "I'll pick something up on the way home."

"See that you do." Juana grabbed up her coat and purse. "Getting nippy out there tonight. Take care. I'll see you in the morning."

"'Night." Bren was barely aware of the door closing as she returned her attention to the lengthy document.

The hour dragged into two, and then three, before she finally pushed away from her desk. Pressing a hand to the small of her back she straightened before walking to the closet to retrieve her trenchcoat and handbag. Her footsteps echoed in the silent halls. At the door she bade good-night to the familiar guard, then made her way to her car in the parking garage. Minutes later she was heading toward the apartment she kept in the heart of D.C. Though she still managed to make it to her mother's place in Chevy Chase at least once or twice a week, she found herself spending more and more time in her apartment, in order to avoid having to deal with morning traffic.

When she passed a small convenience store, she was tempted to stop, but the thought of going home, getting out of her office clothes and into something comfortable was too tempting. She drove to her apartment complex and pulled into an empty parking slot. As she stepped out of her car she was thinking about making tea and toast and climbing into bed to watch the late news.

Smiling at the thought, she headed toward the elevator. Before she could push the button a figure stepped out of the shadows. Too late, Bren realized it was a man, looming over her. In his hand was a pistol.

"Your purse." The two words were spoken in a tortured rasp.

"Yes. Here." She thrust it toward him, her gaze riveted on the gun. She started to back away but his hand snaked out, catching her by the wrist and hauling her close.

"Not so fast."

She nearly gagged at the stench of his fetid breath and unwashed body and clothes.

"I'll take that gold chain." He tore it from

her neck with such force it broke, sending the small diamond pendant sailing through the air.

He swore viciously. ''Now the earrings.''

With trembling hands she reached up and pulled them free, dropping them into his palm.

He gave a nervous, jittery laugh that sent ice skittering down her spine as he took aim. ''Thanks. For nothing.''

In that split second Bren thought about her father. He'd faced death with courage and dignity. As his daughter, she would do no less. She lifted her head a fraction and stared into the stranger's eyes, refusing to beg or plead, knowing it would only feed his sickness.

As his finger closed around the trigger he was suddenly jerked backward with such force, he was caught completely off guard. At the same instant, the gun was yanked roughly from his hands and tossed aside.

''Okay. You want to hurt somebody?'' A tall, rugged man dressed in jeans and a denim jacket sent him a blow that had him staggering backward.

''Why you—'' For a moment the gunman shook his head and seemed to sway. Then, realizing he was fighting for his life, he gave a hoarse cry and lowered his head, using it to drive the stranger against the closed doors of the elevator.

Bren watched helplessly as the two men exchanged brutal, punishing blows until, in a final thrust, the denim-clad man drove the gunman up against the concrete wall of the parking garage. With his breath coming hard and fast he pounded the gunman's head again and again until, battered into unconsciousness, the gunman slid to the floor.

Keeping an eye on him the man pulled a cell phone from his pocket. "Stevens? Banning. Send a black-and-white to the Middlegate Apartments. Got a coke-head in the parking garage." He glanced over at Bren. "You hurt, miss? Need an ambulance?"

"N-no." She leaned a hand against the wall, suddenly wanting to feel something strong and steady behind her.

Within minutes the sound of sirens grew louder. Two squad cars pulled up, and four uniformed police officers leaped out and greeted the man with friendly calls as they loaded the unconscious attacker into the back of one of the cars.

"Hey, Chris." A smiling young cop saluted. "You just can't get away from it, can you?"

"Looks like it." The stranger strolled closer and spoke with the others.

From the easy camaraderie between him and these officers, Bren realized that her rescuer was one of them.

He turned to where Bren was still leaning weakly against the wall. He held out her purse. "Do you live in this building, or were you here on a visit?"

She clutched the purse to her chest. "I live here."

"All right. Why don't I see you safely to your apartment. When the officers are finished here, one of them will come by and take your statement."

"Yes. That'd be…fine." She watched while he pressed the button. When the elevator doors opened she stepped shakily inside and again leaned against the wall.

He gave her a long, steady look. "You sure you're feeling okay?"

"Just a little light-headed."

"Here." He draped an arm around her shoulders and held her close until the doors glided open.

Bren held herself rigid, fighting the desire to slump against him. The feel of that strong, steady arm around her was so comforting she nearly wept.

Still holding on to her, he moved along beside her down the long hallway and around the bend until she paused in front of her closed door. Her hands were trembling as she fished the key from her purse. He took it from her and opened the door, then paused to snap on lights before leading her across the room to a sofa.

She sank down gratefully. "I owe you my life. He was going to shoot me."

He shrugged off her thanks with modesty. "No telling how somebody will act when they're all hopped up." He rubbed his shoulder. "For a skinny guy, he threw a hell of a punch. They usually do when they're that high."

He glanced around, liking the simple contemporary lines of the place. Her surroundings seemed to suit her. Strong colors. No frills. Despite her small stature, he'd recognized, in that split second before he'd jumped into the fight, the strength in her. She hadn't flinched at the thought of her own death. There had been something heroic about the way she'd faced her attacker.

Now that he had a chance to get a good look at her in the light, she was even more fascinating than he'd thought. A short cap of red curls framed a face as pale as porcelain. The only thing that saved her from being movie-star gorgeous was the dusting of freckles across her nose. Her eyes were the most unusual shade of blue green. There was a huskiness to her voice that made it appealing. He hadn't decided if it was nerves, or if that was the way she always sounded. At any rate, he found it incredibly sexy.

There was no ring on her finger.

"My name's Chris."

"Bren."

"Bren." He nodded toward the wet bar across the room. "If you have some brandy or whiskey, it might take the edge off those nerves."

She looked embarrassed. "I'm not sure what's in there. I haven't had occasion to use it yet. But you can check."

He opened a cabinet and studied the unopened bottles. "You live alone, Bren? Or is there a roommate?"

"I live alone."

He felt a ripple of satisfaction as he held up a bottle. "Here's some fine Irish whiskey. Guaranteed to take the edge off anything."

"It was a gift from my grandfather."

"Really? He's got good taste." He poured a liberal amount into a tumbler and crossed the room to hand it to her.

As she accepted it she asked, "Aren't you having any?"

"No, thanks. I have an appointment. As soon as one of the officers gets here, I have to be on my way."

Just then there was a knock on the door, and he hurried to admit one of the uniformed officers. The two spoke quietly for several minutes before Chris turned.

"This is Officer Tom Reed. He'll take your statement. If there's anybody you'd like him to call to stay with you tonight..."

Bren was already shaking her head. "That won't be necessary." She held up the glass of whiskey. "If I drink all this, I'll be out as soon as my head hits the pillow."

"Okay. If you're sure." He turned away.

Before he could leave, Bren called, "Thanks

again, Chris. I'm sure you know how grateful I am.''

He shot her a brilliant smile. ''My pleasure.'' He pulled open the door and noted the alarm system blinking on a wall monitor. ''Make sure you set this.''

Bren watched until the door closed. Then she took a deep breath and began answering the officer's questions, watching as he recorded everything in his official report.

When he stood to leave she cleared her throat. ''I know a simple thank you doesn't sound like much. But it comes from my heart.''

''You're welcome, ma'am. I'm just glad this one had a happy ending.''

''Thanks to Chris.''

The police officer pulled open the door and nodded toward the blinking light of the security monitor. ''I hope you'll do as he asked and set your alarm. After what you've been through, you're bound to feel a little wired.''

''Thanks. I will.''

As soon as he was gone, Bren hurried across the room and bolted the door before punching in the security code.

Half an hour later she lay in her bed in the

dark and began to relive everything that had happened tonight. Each time she closed her eyes she could see her attacker. Could see the jittery movements as he waved the gun in her face. Could even smell him, until her stomach clenched and she cried out.

She sat up and turned on the light, knowing she would need its comfort throughout the night. She mounded the pillows and leaned back, thinking about the stranger who had saved her life. If Chris hadn't come along, she knew with complete certainty that she wouldn't have survived.

For the first time since that awful ordeal had begun, she gave in to the need to weep.

Chapter 2

"Yeah. Banning here." Chris snatched up the phone on the second ring.

"Sorry to spoil your day off, Chris." The Chief of Police, Roger Martin, had a voice so loud Chris found himself holding the receiver away from his ear. "How would you like to represent the department on *Meet the Media* this morning?"

Despite the fact that he'd been awakened from a sound sleep, Chris managed a laugh. "Do I have a choice?"

"No."

He gave a sigh and sat up, running a hand through his hair.

The chief's voice boomed. "I just had a call inviting our department to send someone to debate a freshman congresswoman looking into the excessive use of force by police. I want someone who can think on his feet, Chris, and cut this power-hungry politician down to size."

"Why me? Why don't you handle this, Chief?"

"I'm too mad right now. I'd probably forget my manners and make a fool of myself. Not to mention that I'd probably make an enemy of this congresswoman for life. Besides, your records show that you were the captain of your debating team at Georgetown. I want someone who'll make our position clear to the viewers."

"Does our department have an official position on this?"

"Our Internal Affairs office does a credible job of investigating questionable behavior by one of our own. That's why the office was created. We don't need outside investigators coming in to do the same job. As for firepower, we're against brute force, but in favor of giving our officers every advantage against the criminal element. Hell, if I could give our men and women on the street rocket launchers, I'd do it in a heartbeat.''

The two men shared a laugh.

''Okay.'' Chris got to his feet and started across the room. ''How soon do I have to be at the television studio?''

''They'd like you there within the hour. The show goes on at ten.''

''I'm on my way.'' Chris disconnected as he headed toward the bathroom.

Minutes later he stepped out of the shower and toweled dry before tossing the towel into a hamper. He tore away a plastic dry-cleaning bag and slipped into a perfectly starched shirt. It wouldn't do to show up in a rumpled uniform. As he dressed he found himself thinking about the woman who'd been on his mind most of the night. He loved the cool way she'd handled herself under fire. Most women would have begged and pleaded for mercy. Not that it would have done a bit of good. When a junkie was as high as that one, he was beyond making a rational decision. For a man who was brain-dead, taking a life meant nothing at all.

Chris paused in his routine, eyes narrowed on his own reflection. He couldn't help admiring the way that one small female had been prepared to accept death at the hands of a gunman. That wasn't something that could be taught. There were veteran cops who weren't beyond freezing in fear when confronted by an armed attacker. But that little redhead had held her ground, prepared to accept her fate with courage and dignity. That took real guts.

As he stepped out of his apartment and headed toward the parking garage, he squared his shoulders. At the moment he'd rather be facing an armed coke-head than the grilling he anticipated from the team of reporters on *Meet The Media.*

"Hi, Pop." Bren answered her cell phone as she was shown into the TV studio's green room. She flashed a smile at the production assistant who offered her coffee. "Sorry. I was looking forward to Sunday brunch with the family, but I accepted an invitation to appear on *Meet the Media* instead."

She shook her head when the young assistant offered her cream or sugar. "Black is fine," she whispered in an aside. Then into her phone, ''Sorry. Just getting some much-needed caffeine. Tell the family I'll blow them a kiss on camera.''

When she rang off, the young woman said, ''If you're ready, I'll take you upstairs to makeup.''

''Fine.'' Bren trailed along, grateful that the coffee was hot and strong. After the night she'd put in, she needed all the help she could get. When she hadn't been thinking about her close brush with death, her sleep had been disturbed just thinking about the denim-clad angel who'd saved her life. When she had time to get her wits about her, she'd find out his full name and then find a way to properly thank him and the others in his department who had responded so quickly.

''Here you are, Ms. Lassiter.'' The young assistant ushered her into a room occupied by a smiling woman in a smudged smock. ''Val will do your hair and makeup.''

Val pointed with her comb. ''If you'll take a seat here I'll have a look in my bag of tricks.''

Bren sank into the chair and set her coffee aside.

Val lifted a strand of her hair. "Great color."

"Thanks."

"Who did it?"

Bren couldn't help chuckling. "Nature."

"You don't say." Val joined in the laughter. "Lucky you." She touched a hand to her own hair, streaked with purple. "The rest of us have to help Mother Nature along." She began opening jars and pots, blending colors into the palm of her hand.

Seeing it, Bren arched a brow. "I'd like to look as natural as possible."

"I understand. But the studio lights would wash you out without the proper makeup." As the woman talked she began adding foundation, a bit of color to Bren's cheeks, some creamy eyeshadow. After sponging muted color on her lips she picked up a comb and teased a few curls before saying, "There you go, Congresswoman. On camera this makeup won't even show. All the audience at home will see is your pretty face."

Bren grinned. "I'd rather the audience would pay attention to what I say."

"Then just flash them that big smile, and you'll have them eating out of your hand."

Bren chuckled. "Promise?"

"Yeah." Val glanced up as the production assistant returned. "Right on time. Ten minutes to showtime, and I still have one more guest to get ready."

The young woman juggled an armload of notes. "If you'll follow me, Ms. Lassiter, I'll take you into the studio now."

In the doorway Bren turned to Val. "Thanks for your help. Even if I make a fool of myself out there, at least I know I'll look good."

"That you will, Congresswoman. Happy to oblige."

Bren followed the assistant to the studio where the moderators were already seated at a round table. After greeting each of them, she took her assigned seat and a member of the crew came forward to attach the microphone to her lapel.

A floor manager was giving last-minute directions to the cameramen. He, in turn, was getting his orders through an earphone from the director who was seated with the technicians in a booth to one side.

Above the din a voice came through a speaker. "Is the police chief here yet?"

The moderator shook his head. "Chief Martin isn't coming. He's sending one of his officers. A Captain Banning."

The floor manager turned to Bren. "We're doing a mike check. The director would like you to say a few words."

Bren cleared her throat. "Good morning. My name is..."

He nodded. "Thanks. That'll do." He called out, "One minute to show time, ladies and gentlemen. Where's our other guest?"

"Coming now," the production assistant shouted from the doorway.

"Get the lead out," came a booming voice as a member of the crew stepped up to attach the last microphone.

The floor manager began counting down, and silence settled over the room.

Bren watched as the crew member stepped aside, revealing the face of their other guest.

She let out a gasp and was grateful that the camera was trained on the moderator. Otherwise, all around the country, she would have been seen in a moment of absolute, jaw-dropping astonishment.

She was only vaguely aware of the moderator's voice making the introductions.

"Our guests this morning come from opposite sides of a very hot topic here in Washington this week. Congresswoman Mary Brendan Lassiter and D.C. Police Captain Christopher Banning."

The moderator turned to her. "Congresswoman, you gave an impassioned speech yesterday, in which you called for an independent investigation of our police force, and made a plea to limit the amount of force a police officer may use in the pursuit of his duty."

She managed a smile. "I'm afraid that's a bit simplistic, David. I did say that if the public is unhappy with the results of an investigation of the force by its Internal Affairs Department, it ought to be followed up by an independent investigation. I wouldn't care if that were done by a government agency, or even one launched by one of the city's newspapers, as long as it would uncover the facts. As for limiting firepower, consider this—if even one innocent person is harmed while a police officer is pursuing duty, that's one person too many. I believe our police can go about their jobs without causing death and destruction to the people they're being paid to protect."

The moderator turned to Chris. "How would you respond to that, Captain Banning?"

"I would have to say I agree with the congresswoman. The last thing a police officer wants is to bring harm to the innocent." Chris kept his hands carefully folded atop the table and kept his smile in place. But just barely. He was still in a state of shock. If anyone had told him that the gorgeous redhead who had cost him a night's sleep was Congresswoman Mary Brendan Lassiter, he'd have burst into a fit of laughter. With that shiny cap of red curls and those laughing eyes, she looked more like a perky model pitching mouthwash or herbal shampoo. She was the absolutely last person he'd expected to see sitting across from him during a televised debate. "We take great pride in our work. We realize that it isn't for the faint of heart."

"So." The moderator turned to his colleague with a look of puzzlement. "It seems that instead of a debate, we have like minds on the subject."

"Hardly." Chris saw the camera return to his face. "Though we may agree on our goals, we certainly disagree on how to attain them. Anything that limits the ability of a police officer to carry out his mission with a maximum of safety should be soundly rejected by our citizens. As for allowing an independent agency to investigate our force, I see that as overkill. That's exactly what our Internal Affairs Department is paid to do.''

The moderator seemed absolutely delighted. It occurred to Bren that if he were off camera, he'd probably be rubbing his hands in glee. Still, she couldn't help rising to the challenge.

''I'm sure Captain Banning wants to assure his men and women as much safety as is humanly possible. As do I. But not at the expense of civilians. The men and women who serve as police officers are highly trained. Not so our citizens. The average person has no defense against high-speed chases on our highways, or high-powered assault rifles being discharged into a crowd. What I called for on the floor of the House, and what my committee is investigating, is a common-sense approach to police work in our community and around the country. We don't necessarily want to curb their firepower. But we do want to rein in those few who abuse their power. I believe that our police officers should be given basic sensitivity training, so that they are more open to the needs of the community. And when they violate basic sensitivity, they should be open to a thorough investigation. I disapprove of the code of silence that prevents honest, decent members of the police force from revealing the identity of fellow officers who choose the path of dishonesty. If our citizens don't accept the credibility of Internal Affairs, they should have the right to demand an open and honest investigation of the department.''

Chris saw the heads of several of the media nodding in agreement. He would give her this much. She could be very persuasive. But then, so could he. Which was why the chief had given him this assignment.

He kept his tone reasonable. ''Though I agree that we need to be sensitive to the needs of the people we serve, I must emphasize that anything that ties the hands of our officers also threatens the safety of our citizens. The only thing that stands between your safety and the violence of the street is the enforcement of law. Your police officer is that enforcer. As my chief said, ''If I could give my men and women on the force rocket launchers, I would.''

There was a smattering of laughter, and the

moderator took that moment to call for a commercial break.

As the cameras cut away, an assistant approached Bren. ''Our moderator wants you to know that you'll be allotted one full minute for a closing argument.''

Bren watched as another assistant spoke to Chris. The two shared an easy laugh. Apparently he was as cool and composed under this kind of fire as he'd been last night under a very different sort. She sighed and realized the young woman was waiting for her response. ''Give David my thanks. One minute ought to do nicely.''

When the young woman walked away, Bren looked over to see Chris staring at her. She gave a slight nod of her head in acknowledgment. That brought a smile to his lips before he returned his attention to the floor manager, who was signaling that the show was about to continue.

As the camera technicians moved into position, Bren wondered how much longer she could keep her smile in place. She'd been looking forward to giving the voters her side of this issue. *Meet the Media* was considered the perfect vehicle for such things, and, like her colleagues, she'd leaped at the opportunity to appear. But now it all felt flat. Because of Chris Banning.

That only made her want to try even harder to get her point across. She hadn't come here to be beaten down by a good-looking, smooth-talking sharpie in a cop's uniform.

She'd always been a sucker for a man in uniform. It probably came from her hero worship of her dad. And this man looked so good, he could be a model for a recruitment poster. Razor-short dark hair. Drop-dead-perfect features. Strong, square jaw. A killer smile. And a body that would cause any normal female from eight to eighty to drool.

A question asked of him by one of the media had her snapping to attention.

"Captain Banning, I'm told you are one of the department's youngest, and its most highly decorated, captains. That doesn't come without its share of danger. After your years in the trenches, is it possible to retain your idealism? Or do you become hardened to the realities of life?"

Chris flicked a glance at Bren. "I suppose I'm something of a cynic. After seeing the seamiest side of life, there's a certain amount of grit on my rose-colored glasses.''

"And you, Congresswoman Lassiter? I see by your bio that you are the granddaughter of a police lieutenant, and the daughter of a police officer who died in the line of fire. Shouldn't those things make you even more eager to boost the weapons of our police, rather than limit their access to high-powered weapons?''

Bren saw Chris straighten and stare directly at her. He looked as surprised as she'd been earlier. At least that was one point in her favor.

"I did lose my father, Riordan Lassiter, in the line of duty. And I'm reminded daily just how precious life is. Because of a carefully aimed bullet from a high-powered rifle, and one moment frozen in time, I had to grow up without the man I loved more than my own life. I want our police to be the best-equipped, the safest in the world. But at the same time I want our citizens to feel equally safe, not only from criminals, but from those officers who react in a careless manner with weapons that can destroy life. I believe that it's possible for our police and our citizens to find a common ground.''

While Bren had been speaking, the moderator had been handed a piece of paper, which he quickly scanned. Now he looked up sharply. "According to the wire services, you were accosted at gunpoint last night in your apartment parking garage, Congresswoman Lassiter. Is that correct?"

She felt her face flaming. "It is. But I hadn't realized it made the news."

"And why not? It isn't every night that a member of our own Congress is attacked at gunpoint. How did you escape unharmed?"

"I had help from a stranger."

The moderator nodded and tapped a finger on the paper. "According to this, your rescuer was none other than Captain Banning."

Bren nodded, aware that there was no point in trying to make light of the incident, now that the news had been leaked. "At the time, I didn't know his name. In fact, it wasn't until today, on this show, that I learned of his identity."

The moderator turned to Chris. "And you, Captain Banning? Did you know that you'd saved the life of one of our members of Congress?"

Chris shook his head. "I was just glad to be of assistance."

One of the other members of the panel asked, "Does this change your mind about limiting the use of police weapons, Ms. Lassiter?"

"Not at all. In fact, as I recall, Captain Banning never used his weapon. Unless you want to call his fists weapons."

"Apparently they were adequate," the reporter deadpanned.

There was a smattering of laughter.

The moderator turned to Chris. "Because of the time this breaking-news item took, it looks like you'll get the last word, Captain Banning."

Chris looked over at Bren, reading her discomfort. "It's easy to see that Congresswoman Lassiter is sincere. And I applaud her for that. I disagree with the politicians who make pretty speeches and then retreat to the comfort of their ivory towers."

Bren flinched, knowing that was exactly how many of the viewers would see her. Had it been deliberate on his part, just to leave that impression? Or had it been an innocent comment?

"But however well intentioned the congresswoman's motives, she seems to be straddling the fence. She wants it both ways. Open our doors to scrutiny by both the press and the public and risk leaking important information better kept under wraps by our Internal Affairs investigators. Collar the police, keep them on a leash, but insist that they continue to keep our citizens safe. Sorry. That's playing right into the hands of the criminal. The court is the proper venue for protecting the rights of both criminal and victim. But don't restrict the police while they try to do their job. Don't tie the hands of the ones who put their lives on the line every day for your safety."

The floor manager signaled the moderator, who shot a brilliant smile at the camera. "That's all for this week's segment of *Meet the Media*. Our thanks to Congresswoman Mary Brendan Lassiter and Captain Christopher Banning for contributing to a lively debate."

There was another moment of silence, and then, while the crew began moving cables and stashing microphones, Bren and Chris were surrounded by the members of the press who had formed the panel.

"Fine job, Ms. Lassiter."

"Thank you."

"And you, Captain Banning. You had us worried that you wouldn't make it."

"Sorry. There was an…incident on my way here."

"Don't tell me you stumbled onto another armed attack on a civilian?"

That brought a round of laughter from the assembled.

"No. Sorry. I don't usually get more than two or three of those a day." Chris smiled easily. "Just a minor traffic accident. As soon as help arrived on the scene, I was able to leave. Thanks again for having me here to express the views of my department."

Seeing Bren taking her leave, he started across the studio.

Before Bren could shut the door he was beside her, matching his pace to hers. "How about stopping for some coffee? I'll even allow you to try your powers of persuasion on me."

It was on the tip of her tongue to refuse. But there was just something about his smile that had her heart doing a slow dip. He put a hand under her elbow and began steering her toward the parking lot.

Something perverse in her nature had her flashing that warm Lassiter smile. "Why not? My car or yours?"

Chapter 3

Chris held the door of his car open while Bren settled herself inside. Then he rounded the car and slid behind the wheel.

He flashed her another heart-stopping smile. "I know a place where they make the best omelets in town."

"You just said the magic word."

"Ah. A woman after my own heart." He put the car in gear and headed into light traffic. "I was afraid, judging by that perfect figure, that you might be one of those women who eat nothing but berries and twigs."

She was still reacting from his remark about

her figure when her cell phone rang. She fished it from her shoulder bag. "Hello."

Hearing the voice on the line, she fell silent a moment before saying, "Sorry, Pop. I know I should have called you last night. But I needed some time." After another pause she said softly, "I didn't plan on having my entire family learn about it from a TV show. But I'm fine. Really." She sighed. "All right. I'll talk to her."

She took in a deep breath before saying, "Hi, Mom. Yes, I'm fine. It was very frightening. But it's over now. No, I won't be by until later today. I'm…going to breakfast right now with Captain Banning." She paused and glanced at Chris, who kept his eyes on the highway. "Yes, I'll tell him. Bye now."

She tucked her phone in her bag. "My mother sends you her thanks."

"All in a day's work. I take it your family's a little upset?"

"To put it mildly." Bren shrugged. "She and my grandfather weren't too happy to hear the news on TV before I'd had a chance to tell them."

"I can't blame them for that. Why didn't you phone them last night?"

"Because I knew this would be their reaction. They're being overprotective, as always. Now they don't want me to spend another night alone in my apartment. They both think I'd be better off staying with them for a while."

"Maybe they're right."

She sighed. "In case you haven't noticed, I'm a big girl now."

Chris gave her a look that had the heat rising to her cheeks. "Oh, yeah, I've noticed."

He turned into the parking lot of a graceful white building with green canopies over tall, floor-to-ceiling windows. It looked more like a cozy country cottage than a restaurant.

They were greeted at the door by a smiling hostess who called Chris by name. "You're late, Captain Banning. You're usually our first customer."

"Yeah. I had to take care of a tough assignment this morning." He winked at Bren as they were led to a table for two overlooking a pretty patio where autumn leaves drifted from a towering oak.

After filling their cups with steaming coffee and handing them menus, the hostess left them alone.

Chris had no need to read the menu. He set it aside before lifting his head to study Bren. "Why didn't you tell me you were in Congress?"

Bren managed a laugh. "I guess I was a bit overwhelmed. It was the first time I'd ever faced an armed man. My brain cells were temporarily frozen. Why didn't you tell me you were a police captain?"

"Must have slipped my mind."

She tossed her head. "I doubt that too much gets past that steel-trap mind of yours. You were a formidable foe on *Meet the Media*."

"That's what the chief was hoping. Of course, he's well aware that I was captain of my debate team at Georgetown." He sipped his coffee. "Where'd you do your debating?"

"What makes you think I did?"

"You're too good."

She laughed. "Okay. You caught me. Princeton. We took top honors my senior year."

"With you as captain, no doubt."

She nodded. Her smile faded as she ran her finger around and around the rim of her cup. "I don't mean to make light of what happened last night. My mother isn't the only one who's grateful, Chris. I never properly thanked you for saving my life.''

''My pleasure, ma'am.''

She gave an involuntary shudder. ''When I think what might have happened...''

He laid a hand over hers, stilling her movements. ''Don't go there. There's nothing to be gained by playing that mind game. It's over now. That's what's important.''

''I know.'' At the touch of his hand she felt a quick rush of heat and wondered if he did, too. ''I did enough of that last night.''

''You should have taken my advice and phoned someone to come over and keep you company.''

She nodded. ''In hindsight, I know you're right. But I hated the thought of someone hovering over me all night long.''

His smile was quick and dangerous. ''I'll bet there are a dozen guys who'd fight for the privilege.''

Bren laughed. ''Sorry. Only half a dozen that I know of.''

''Give me their names, and I'll have them all arrested.''

They were both laughing when the waitress came to take their order.

When she walked away, Chris drained his coffee cup. "What made you go into politics?"

Bren fiddled with her spoon. "It wasn't planned. I thought briefly about following my grandfather and father into police work."

"Why didn't you?"

"First of all, there's my size."

That had him laughing. "Yeah. I can't think of too many cops who'd want to partner with a pint-size female, even though I must say you'd look great in a uniform."

She joined in his laughter. "Thanks. And then there's my attitude toward guns."

"So why politics?"

"I went to law school, and had every intention of practicing with a firm." She looked up. "My mother went back to law school after my father died, and works as a family advocate in the District. My brother Cameron followed her lead, and though he works full-time in one of the city's top firms, he also works pro bono on a few cases each year. I admire him for that and thought I'd follow suit, but—" she shrugged "—I changed courses after working for Congressman Harrison one summer. I saw the way he fought for his constituents, and the difference one man could make. And when he decided not to run again because of ill health, I jumped in, even though I figured I didn't have a prayer of a chance of winning.''

''Next thing you knew, you were the freshman congresswoman from Maryland.''

''Yeah. I still haven't figured out which hallway leads to which chamber. I'm still trying to complete my staff, and I've already been appointed to my first committee.''

''And making speeches heard around the world.''

She flushed. ''My speech wasn't nearly as tough on the police as it sounded in those newscasts. They took a couple of sound bytes and made it out to be my entire speech.''

He frowned. ''I've had my share of media exposure. They can put some pretty interesting spins on words.''

They fell silent as the waitress arrived with their order.

As they dug into their omelets, Bren sighed. ''Oh, this is wonderful. It may be even better than Pop's.'' Seeing Chris lift an eyebrow she explained, ''My grandfather moved in after my dad was shot, and became our full-time cook, cleaner and housekeeper.''

"Your mom didn't mind?"

Bren shook her head. "She often says that Pop saved her life, and we saved his. We were all in a state of shock. I guess none more than Pop, who'd just buried his only son. My brothers and I gave him a reason to live. And he kept all of us in food and clean clothes. Also in line. No one ever talked back to Kieran Lassiter and lived to tell about it."

"I think I'd like to meet your grandfather."

"You'd like him. And he'd like you."

"How can you tell?"

Her smile was quick. "It's a cop thing."

"Yeah. We do tend to stick together." He smiled at the waitress who topped off their cups before handing him the bill. "I've been meaning to ask. What kind of name is Mary Brendan?"

She laughed. "After two sons, my father expected another boy. Brendan was his grandfather's name. When I was born, he just tacked on Mary, and left it at that."

"And that was fine with your mother?"

Bren nodded. "Anything my father wanted was fine with my mother. Theirs really was a love match."

She saw a strange mix of emotions cross his face before he composed himself.

Minutes later their waitress returned to clear their table and take his credit card.

Chris sat back, obviously content after his meal. "Can you take the rest of the day to play?"

Bren sighed. "I wish. I have so many committee reports to read, I may go blind."

"Sounds like a fun afternoon."

"What about you? Is this a day off?"

"Sort of. It will be after I drop by the office to complete last night's report and go over the interrogation of your attacker. I figure by now he's probably climbing the walls of his cell and hoping a lawyer can get him out so he can get a hit of something to take the edge off."

Bren looked alarmed. "They won't release him, will they?"

Chris lay a hand over hers. "Relax. Now that it's all over the news that he attacked a member of our esteemed Congress, there's no chance a judge will let him out on bail."

She gave a visible sigh of relief.

"Come on." Chris held her chair before leading the way across the room.

Outside, the air had a bite to it, even though the sun had burst through the clouds.

As Chris turned the ignition and headed back to the television studio, Bren studied his hands on the wheel. There was such power in them. When he'd come to her rescue, he'd become, in that moment, her white knight. She could swear she'd heard her attacker's bones snapping like twigs. When it was over, she'd wanted, more than anything, to fling herself into this man's arms and beg him to hold her.

Safe. When he'd dropped an arm around her in the elevator, she'd felt as though nothing could possibly harm her.

"Here we are."

She looked up to see that they were already in the parking lot of the TV studio. Chris came around and held her door while offering his hand.

She had no choice but to put her hand in his. At once she felt the sizzle of heat along her arm. She kept her smile in place. "Thanks for breakfast."

"You're welcome." Instead of moving back, he remained where he was, so that their bodies were almost touching. "I'd like to see you again. Is there someone significant in your life?''

She decided to keep it light. ''Well, you know about my mother and grandfather. I also have three brothers and two sisters-in-law. Is that enough significant people in one life?''

''Yeah. More than enough. And none of them what I'd consider competition.''

''You don't like competition?''

''I thrive on it. But I'm not interested in another man's woman.'' His hands were moving along her arms, sending the most delicious tingles along her spine. ''And now that I know there isn't a husband or significant other...''

Without warning he laid a hand on her cheek and stared deeply into her eyes as he brushed her lips with his. It was the merest touch of mouth to mouth, but he saw her eyes widen before the lashes fluttered, then closed. Heard her little sigh of surprise before her breath mingled with his and her lips softened, then opened to him.

Sensing her compliance, his arms came around her, dragging her firmly against him. His mouth covered hers in a kiss that had the breath backing up in her throat.

His lips were warm and firm as they moved

over hers, taking with a possessiveness that shocked her. What shocked her even more was her response. A sound like a whimper escaped her throat. She reached a hand to his chest to hold him at bay. The next thing she knew, her fingers were curled into the front of his shirt, drawing him even closer.

She wanted desperately to wrap herself around him. To feel that strong, muscled body against hers. Instead she forced herself to stand very still. But though her body obeyed her, her mind refused. In the space of a single kiss, she could feel her focus beginning to blur. Could feel her mind emptying and her body straining toward his.

When at last he lifted his head, she had to take several deep breaths until she was able to gather her thoughts.

He took her hand, linking his fingers with hers.

She shot him a look of astonishment.

He merely smiled and led her toward her car. When he had the door opened he settled her inside, then leaned close. He saw her eyes widen. That only made him smile all the more.

''I'll call you.'' His warm breath feathered

the hair at her temple and sent an odd little tingle down her spine.

"I have an unlisted number."

He gave her a smile that had her heart taking a hard, quick bounce before doing a dance in her chest. "Then I'll just have to knock on your door one of these nights."

"I put in long hours on committee meetings."

"I'll come over afterward and we can debate the effect of sensitivity training on overzealous police officers."

"That's not my idea of a fun evening."

"Give me a chance to change your mind."

"About sensitivity training? Hardly."

"Well then, at least about the fun part." He leaned in, until his mouth brushed hers. "Did I tell you that I do my best debating while rubbing my opponent's back?" He kissed her again, keeping it as light as an autumn breeze. "Or feet." One more feathery kiss as he whispered, "Or other parts of the anatomy. Goodbye, Mary Brendan Lassiter."

She heard the car door close. Watched as he walked back to his own car and started the engine. And though she mechanically fastened her seat belt and turned the key in the ignition, her mind was still spinning in endless circles.

She waited until he'd driven away before lowering the windows and breathing deeply. Then, putting the car in gear, she started toward her apartment. All the way there she wondered just how all that had happened. One minute they were having a leisurely breakfast and a few laughs. The next they were acting like long-lost lovers.

Lovers.

She touched a fingertip to her lips. She could still feel the imprint of his mouth on hers. Could still taste him. So dark and male and…potent.

She shook her head to clear her mind. What she needed was a good dose of reality to bring her back to earth. And she knew just the thing—the endless pages of her latest committee report that needed to be digested before the start of another work week.

Chapter 4

"Pop?" Bren was busy stuffing papers into her already bulging briefcase as she rested her cell phone between shoulder and ear. "I'm really sorry about missing dinner again tonight. It couldn't be helped. Two of our committee members had to juggle their schedules, and this was the only night we were all available. So tell me what I missed."

With her grandfather's voice buzzing in her ear, she waved a hand to the cleaning crew as she swept from the office and along the almost deserted hallway. At the entrance she paused to smile at the night guard before hurrying to her car.

Inside, she tossed aside her briefcase and turned the key in the ignition, all the while making appropriate sounds of pleasure as Kieran Lassiter described the stuffed pork chops, the garlic mashed potatoes and the lemon chiffon pie her family had enjoyed in her absence.

"Stop." She laughed. "Do you know what I've had to eat all day? A cafe latte around seven this morning, and a wilted salad at my desk sometime around midday." She sighed as she turned into her apartment complex and found an empty slot. Before stepping out of her car she took a moment to peer around for any sign of movement. It had only been days since the attack, and each night when she arrived back here she found her heart rate speeding up and her adrenaline pumping through her veins at the thought of navigating the dimly lit parking structure.

Was that why she kept her grandfather talking? Was she subconsciously in need of company until she reached the safety of her own apartment?

With his voice still humming in her ear she scooped up her briefcase and stepped out of her car. "Yes, the thought of a midnight snack of leftovers is tempting, Pop. But I still have a ton of paperwork to finish. I'll have to take a rain check. But I promise you, I'll make it over before the end of the week."

She pressed the elevator button and turned to stare around at the parked cars. When the elevator doors slid silently open, she stepped inside and pressed the button to her floor. "Tell Mom and Cam I send my love, Pop."

She tucked the cell phone into her coat pocket and stepped off at her floor. As she started along the corridor, she heard a footfall behind her. She stopped and turned. Was that a shadow in that doorway? Or was she letting her imagination get the best of her?

She resolutely started forward again, only to feel the hair at the back of her neck rising. She could sense someone behind her. She quickened her pace and could feel the footsteps behind her picking up the pace, as well.

Her breath was coming hard and fast as she rounded the corner toward her apartment. Blindly digging into her pocket for the key, she looked up just in time to see a tall shadowy figure standing outside her door. Before she could halt her momentum, she slammed into him.

Her breath came out in a whoosh of air.

"Chris." She started to push away but he caught her by the upper arms and stared down into her eyes. Eyes wide with terror.

His voice was gruff. "What's wrong?"

"I thought…" She took a moment to suck in a breath. "Just nerves, I know. But I thought I sensed somebody following me."

"Go inside." Without waiting he took her key and fitted it into the lock, shoving her inside. "I'll be right back. Don't open the door until you hear my voice."

By the time she'd closed the door, she could hear fast, impatient footsteps receding. A short time later she heard a rap on her door, followed by the sound of his voice.

"It's Chris. Open up."

Bren peered through the peephole, then threw the safety lock and stood aside.

"Nobody there?"

He shook his head.

She gave a shaky laugh. "I've always been cursed with an overactive imagination. Pop used to say I was too fanciful for my own good."

"Don't put yourself down." He touched a hand to her arm and felt her jerk back. Nerves. She was so wired she was jangling. "I believe in trusting my instincts. You should, too."

She ran a hand through her hair. "I've got to get over it. I can't believe how jumpy I've been since that..." She turned away, clearly annoyed with herself. "I've never been a timid mouse. I'm not going to start now."

She turned back, her smile in place. "If I hadn't been so distracted, I would have asked sooner. What are you doing here? Not that I mind. I was awfully glad to see a familiar face after running into you."

"I told you I'd come knocking on your door. Since this was my first free night in a week, I thought I'd spend it with you."

"Just like that? Without calling first?"

"I tried your office number. One of your staff took my name and number and said you were tied up, but you never called back."

"Sorry." She flushed. "I left my office this afternoon for a committee meeting. By the time I returned, it was so late I didn't even bother to look through my messages."

"Yeah, well, since you have an unlisted

number here, I thought I'd just take a chance on catching you in. Have you eaten?''

"No. As a matter of fact I—''

"Good.'' He turned away and opened her door, bending down to retrieve something. When he straightened, he was holding two handled shopping bags.

"What's all this?''

"Dinner.'' He moved past her to the kitchen, where he began removing items from the bags. "I'm about to feed you.''

"Do you need any help?''

He shook his head. "Why don't you go make yourself comfortable. Unless, of course, you like relaxing in those fancy-lady clothes.''

"I'll be right back.'' She made her way to her bedroom and kicked off her shoes. Within minutes she'd removed her suit and replaced it with a russet turtleneck and matching leggings. Tossing her earrings on the dresser top, she walked barefoot to the other room.

He looked up from the kitchen counter where he'd just filled two stem glasses with red wine. "Now that's what I call relaxed.''

Bren gave a throaty laugh. "You did say comfortable.''

He handed her a glass. "I did. And that looks comfortable enough to sleep in."

"I hope you aren't thinking of sticking around to see for yourself."

"A guy can hope, can't he?" He gave her a slow, steady look before turning away.

While he rummaged through the pots and pans in her cupboard, Bren took a moment to sip her wine. The smoldering look he'd given her had her throat as dry as dust.

He held a shiny pan aloft. "Haven't you ever used any of these?"

She shook her head. "No time."

"I thought so. They look like props in a movie. Are you sure it's all right with you if they get dirty?"

"I'm fine with it. In fact, I'll clean up whatever mess you make, as long as you're willing to feed me."

She set two places at the small, glass-topped table before leaning against the counter and watching in silence as he worked. He looked completely comfortable in her small kitchen, heating water for pasta, sautéing onions and green pepper in a skillet. Soon the room was perfumed with the wonderful aroma of rolls dusted with Parmesan cheese, and veal in a light wine sauce.

He lifted the bottle of wine and topped off their glasses. "I didn't cook the veal or the pasta sauce. I picked it up at one of my favorite Italian restaurants. The owner, Tony, is an old friend. But I think you'll like it."

"As long as I don't have to cook it, I guarantee I'll love it." She sipped her wine and sighed. "Most career women covet a good cleaning staff. I'd settle for a live-in cook. Interested?"

"I could be." He gave her another of those steamy looks that were guaranteed to send her heartbeat soaring. "It would depend on the perks of the job. Could I get to see what my boss wears to bed?"

She managed a laugh, despite the fact that she wasn't certain he was kidding. "Sorry. The only guys who ever got to see what I wore while sleeping were my brothers."

"I'm not your brother, Bren." He touched a finger to her cheek. Just a touch, but it sent heat streaking straight to her core. "In fact, if your brothers knew what I was thinking right now, they'd draw straws to see which of them could have the pleasure of tearing off my hide.''

"You don't know my brothers. They wouldn't waste time drawing straws. You'd have to fight off all three of them at once.''

"Tough guys, are they?''

"Yeah. You should have seen some of my poor unlucky dates back in high school and college. Not only did they have to pass muster with my three brothers, but then they had to deal with Pop.''

"I suppose it's harder for a grandfather to accept that his little girl is growing up than it is for a father.''

She nodded. "If Pop had his way, I'd still be considered too young to go out on dates.''

"How old are you?''

She rolled her eyes. "Twenty-eight. Just saying that gives me shivers.''

He laughed. "Try saying thirty-five and single.'' He turned away to drain the pasta, before arranging it on a plate.

Bren watched the slow, easy way he moved. Like a cat. Nothing hurried or rushed. He lifted two salads from the counter and carried them to the table. Then he returned to the stove to pour sauce over the pasta, before bringing it to the table.

If she'd thought him handsome in a uniform, he looked even better in faded denims and a T-shirt. The muscles of his back and upper arms flexed as he set down the platter and turned toward the stove. Minutes later he set a plate of steaming veal in wine sauce and looked over at her.

"Dinner's ready, Ms. Lassiter."

When she walked to the table he was holding her chair. She sat and felt his hand brush her shoulder. He allowed it to linger a moment longer before taking the place across from her.

She glanced over, wondering if he knew what his touch did to her. Judging by the smile on his face, he knew exactly what he was doing. Now if only she did.

She tasted the salad, then looked up in surprise. "This is good. I want that restaurant's dressing."

"The only thing the restaurant supplied is the veal and sauce. I make my own dressing."

She narrowed her eyes at him. "I'm finding this a little hard to believe."

He shrugged. "Suit yourself." He spooned pasta onto her plate, then added thin slices of veal. "Try the pesto sauce. I added my own touch to it. You're going to love it."

She tasted, then gave a murmur of approval.

Chris couldn't help smiling at the look on her face as she emptied her plate and helped herself to seconds.

"When's the last time you ate?"

"Like this? Days ago. Maybe weeks or more. Oh, Chris, this is fantastic."

He sat back grinning. "Well, Ms. Lassiter, I believe I'm going to enjoy cooking for you."

"I'm betting you learned how to do all these fancy things in the kitchen at some expensive prep school. Am I right?"

"Why a prep school?"

She laughed. "It's not something you can hide, Chris Banning. You just have the look of a preppie."

He drained his glass of wine, weighing his answer carefully. Then with a shrug he stood and began clearing the table. "I've been cooking for myself since I was a twelve-year-old kid with nobody to lean on."

Bren opened the dishwasher and began loading the dirty dishes as he handed them to her. "Where were your parents?"

"Gone." He gave a grim laugh. "Not for

the first time. They used to take off periodi-
cally, leaving my sister and me to fend for
ourselves. But when I was twelve they never
came back.''

Puzzled, Bren dried her hands on a kitchen
towel. ''How old was your sister?''

''Marti was fourteen. But tough enough and
savvy enough to make herself look about eighteen, so we were able to fool the social work-
ers and the neighbors for quite a while before
we were found out.''

''Then what happened?''

''We were put into foster care. They
couldn't find anyone willing to take on two
obstinate teens, so Marti was placed in one
home, while I was sent halfway across the city
to another.''

''Did you get to see each other?''

''Only when we ran away. Which was often. But we were always caught and sent back.
The last time we made a pact that as soon as
Marti was old enough she'd come for me, and
we'd never be apart again.''

''I can understand that.'' Bren carefully
draped the towel over the edge of the sink and
thought about the feelings she had for her
brothers. ''If I'd been separated from my fam-

ily, it would have broken my heart. To say nothing of my spirit.'' She looked over at him. ''How did you survive?''

He shrugged. ''I counted the days, the weeks, the months, until Marti and I would get our own place together and get on with our lives. I focused all my energy on that goal.''

She smiled. ''When you're twelve, the waiting can seem interminable.''

He nodded. ''But I found ways to pass the time. Mostly by getting into as much trouble as possible. And then one day my foster parents told me that Marti had run away again. This time the authorities didn't find her until it was too late.''

Bren saw the bleak look in his eyes and braced herself. ''She was…dead?''

''Of a drug overdose.''

''Oh, Chris.'' She placed a hand over his on the kitchen counter.

He studied it without moving. Then looked up. ''It turned out that she'd been hanging with a tough crowd, staying out all night. I guess that was the last straw for me. I'd been pinning all my hopes on getting out of the system once she turned eighteen, and now I realized I was in for the long haul.''

Bren stayed where she was as he turned away, paced, then leaned a hip against the counter. "I went a little nuts. It started with petty crimes. Shoplifting. Then moved up to bigger things. Grand theft auto. And all before my sixteenth birthday. My foster family wanted nothing more to do with me. They sent me to a youth home, where I met guys who knew even better ways to break the law. That should have been the end of the line for me, except for one thing. Or maybe I should say except for one man. Mike Banning. He was the toughest police sergeant I'd ever come across. I figured he was going to bust me good. Instead, he took me home with him. He and his wife Mary Lou gave me something I'd never dreamed I would have in this lifetime."

Bren arched a brow.

He crossed his arms over his chest. "A real home. They let me know that there wasn't anything I could do that would turn them against me. And they proved it time and again while I worked through enough anger to sink the *Titanic*. They even adopted me, though it took a lot of paperwork to have me made a legal ward of the court first, in order to prove to me that they were in this for a lifetime. I went from being Christopher McAllister to Christopher Banning. I think that's when my anger subsided and I discovered to my surprise that I had a good mind. With almost no effort I could pull down top grades in school." He grinned. "You may think I look like prep school material, but I went to an inner-city school before getting into Georgetown on a scholarship. Mike and Mary Lou told me I could be anything in the world I wanted. They hoped I'd be a guidance counselor or go into social work. But in the end all I really wanted was to be like Mike. So after college I joined the police force."

"Oh, Chris. That's wonderful."

"Yeah. The happy ending." He managed a smile. "It's nice to know that I made them both proud before they died."

"They're both gone?"

He nodded. "Mike fought cancer for more than a year, but the cancer won. After that, I think Mary Lou's heart was too broken to ever mend. So within the year she was gone, too."

"And you're alone now."

"Not for the first time. I've learned it's not the worst thing in the world." He rummaged through the shopping bag and came up with a carton containing two slices of cheesecake drizzled with strawberries.

Bren stared at them a moment, then burst into laughter. "Don't you dare try to tell me you made this yourself."

"You're right. Mine's better. Tony threw this in as a bonus."

"Has Tony been reading my mind?"

"You were craving cheesecake?"

"Desperately." She took a bite while he returned to the kitchen counter and plugged in the coffeemaker.

By the time the coffee was ready, they had both devoured their dessert.

Chris filled two cups and looked over at her. "How do you take this?"

"Black."

He carried the two cups and followed her to the sofa in the other room.

She sipped and sighed. "I'm feeling so much better now."

"Yeah. So am I."

Bren looked over at him. "Did Mike and Mary Lou have any children of their own?"

"No." He stared down into his cup. "It must have been hard for two people who'd spent a lifetime caring for each other to suddenly find themselves with this angry, moody kid in their lives. But they never showed me anything except love and patience." He shook his head. "Sometimes when I'm dealing with gang violence, I find myself knowing that I'd have been one of those punks. I was already headed down that road. If it hadn't been for Mike and Mary Lou, I'd have been one of the lost."

"Did you ever locate your parents?"

She saw a look come into his eyes. A mixture of anger and something she couldn't quite define, but it was frightening to see.

He stretched out his long legs, forcing himself to relax. "I never looked for them. As far as I'm concerned, they no longer exist."

"What would you do if you had to confront them?"

"I've asked myself that question. But I've never come up with the answer. I don't know what I'd do. I hope I never have to find out."

Bren snuggled into the corner of the sofa and leaned her head back, studying him. "Did you call the Bannings Mom and Dad?"

He shook his head. "I guess I figured I was too old for that. I was never very good with affectionate titles. I called them Mike and

Mary Lou.'' He saw Bren stifle a yawn and picked up his empty cup, carrying it to the kitchen.

She got to her feet. ''What are you doing?''

''Getting out of here so you can get some sleep.'' He stopped in front of her. ''Unless, of course, you'd like me to share your bed tonight. Still, I doubt you'd get any sleep.''

She laughed. ''You're awfully sure of yourself, aren't you?''

He drew her close and brushed his mouth over hers. ''You just say the word, and I'll be happy to prove my point.''

''I get your point, Captain.'' She placed her fingers over his mouth to stop him from kissing her again. ''Now I think you'd better get going.''

''Killjoy.'' He held her a short distance away. The smile was suddenly gone from his eyes. ''I wanted you to know the truth about me up front. You have a very public career. One that can be ruined by gossip or even a little spin on the truth. If you don't want to be associated with a guy from the wrong side of the tracks, I'll understand.''

She moved her hand until it was resting lightly on his cheek as she stared up into his eyes. Eyes that were narrowed on her with such a fierce look she felt her heart do a slow, crazy somersault.

"There aren't any tracks running through my neighborhood, Chris. Right ones or wrong ones. I admire you for what you've done with your life."

"And you wouldn't mind if I showed up on your doorstep another night?"

She laughed. "As long as you come bearing food, you're welcome anytime."

He drew her close. Against her mouth he whispered, "Just so you know. I'll want to do a whole lot more than feed you, Bren."

She sighed. "One step at a time."

He kissed her again. Long and slow and deep, until she felt her toes curling and her mind beginning to cloud.

How was it possible for him to take her so high with nothing more than a kiss?

"Consider that the first step." He moved back, breaking contact. Then, without a backward glance, he crossed the room and let himself out.

Leaving Bren staring at the closed door with a dazed expression.

Chapter 5

"**B**ren." Juana Sanchez paused in the doorway of Bren's office. "Congressman Roland Paxton just announced that he's on his way over."

Bren sighed. "Did you tell him I have a twelve-o'clock appointment."

"She did." The congressman's rich baritone had both women looking up in surprise. "But what I have to say won't take long." He stepped past Juana and crossed to Bren's desk, offering a handshake before settling himself in one of the leather chairs that flanked her desk.

He was a tall, handsome man, and well

aware of his appeal to his constituents. He often used that voice and commanding presence to bring recalcitrant members of his party into line whenever they threatened to stray from his often heavy-handed use of power.

Behind him Juana rolled her eyes before closing the door.

He pointed to the newspapers on Bren's desk. "I see you've read about the latest incident between a rogue cop and an innocent citizen."

Bren glanced at the glaring headlines. A witness to a citizen's fatal shooting had sworn that the shooter, though not wearing a uniform, had been driving a police car. An autopsy was scheduled for later today to determine if the bullet was police issue.

"I'm sure all of Washington has heard of it, Roland."

"Then somebody ought to tell our police force. The chief was on television just an hour ago defending his men's actions."

"What did you expect him to do, Roland? Abandon them?"

"He needs to be forthright about the misfits in his outfit. Everybody knows there are men who become police officers for less than honorable reasons.''

''Just as there are politicians who use their power for less than honorable reasons.''

He arched a brow. ''Are you going over to their side, Congresswoman?''

''I didn't realize there were sides in this issue.''

''If you think that, you're a fool.'' He got to his feet. ''And I've concluded that you're no fool, Congresswoman Lassiter. Now, I suggest you have your committee draft some strong language and get it out there to counter the swill the police are feeding our constituents. It's time we put a leash on armed thugs.''

Bren stood as well. ''Armed thugs? I hope you're not intending to use that term to describe our police.''

''If the shoe fits...'' He shrugged. ''Whether it's by accident or by design, innocent citizens of this town are falling victim to gunshots fired by police. If you won't steer your committee to action, I'll find someone who will.''

Her head came up. ''Are you threatening me, Roland?''

He paused with his hand on the door. Turning, he shot her one of his smooth, polished smiles which he'd perfected during his ten years in Congress. "Not a threat, Ms. Lassiter. A warning. I was the one who had you assigned to this committee, knowing your voice, as the daughter of a fallen police hero, would carry a great deal of weight in the community. You serve on that committee at my discretion. Anytime I choose, you can be summarily dismissed. Try not to forget that."

Bren waited until the door closed before slumping down in her chair. Roland Paxton was one of the most powerful members of Congress. She had no doubt he would do exactly as he'd warned.

Hadn't she suspected that the reason she'd been assigned to this committee in the first place was because of her father's reputation? Now Roland Paxton had just confirmed that it had nothing to do with her qualifications and everything to do with her bloodline.

She lifted her hands to rub at her temples, where the beginning of a headache pulsed.

Minutes later Juana poked her head in to say, "You might want to turn on the news."

Bren flicked a switch and watched as a reporter was shown outside police headquarters.

The young woman flashed a smile at the camera before saying, "I'm here with Captain Christopher Banning. Captain Banning, in light of this latest incident, how do you answer the charges made by members of a congressional committee investigating unusual force by your officers?"

"I would hope that everyone would remain calm until all the facts are in. We have our own Internal Affairs investigating this incident."

"There seems to be a great deal of skepticism about the integrity of such an investigation. How do you calm the fears of the citizens of Washington?"

As the camera closed in on his face, Bren could see the muscle of his jaw working. "That won't be an easy task, especially with the media, and now a congressional committee, all stirring the pot and vying for airtime."

"Are you suggesting that the members of our Congress are doing this for publicity?"

"Of course not. At least, not all of them. But there are always those few people who take up the latest cause, hoping for their fifteen minutes of fame. But I'm confident that the public will withhold judgment until all the facts are in.''

As the news segment ended, Bren closed her eyes. After that veiled attack on their integrity, her committee members would be even more thirsty for blood.

Her headache was now a full-blown migraine. She gulped a couple of pills before snatching up her attaché case. The work of Congress couldn't be put off because of a little pain.

But as she worked her way through a day filled with paperwork, committee meetings and endless speeches on the floor of the House, she found herself questioning the wisdom of her choice of career.

By the time she was able to return to her office, her staff had left for the day. She found stacked neatly on her desk more than a dozen messages. As she flipped through them, one name and number had her going very still.

Without giving herself time to think, she picked up the phone and dialed the number.

"Captain Banning."

At the sound of his voice, Bren found herself smiling for the first time in hours. "Good evening, Captain. I have a message to call you as soon as possible.''

''Bren.'' He sat back in his chair. ''I was just cleaning up some paperwork. Are you heading back to your apartment now?''

''Yeah.'' She glanced at the file folders littering her desktop. ''The sooner the better.''

''Good. Why don't I meet you there?''

She was already shaking her head. ''I don't think that's a good idea, Chris. It's been a long day.''

''All the more reason to let me come over. I'll feed you.''

''Food.'' She let out a long, slow sigh. ''How soon can you be there?''

He laughed. ''I'm on my way.''

She set down the receiver and started shoving paperwork into her attaché case. Half an hour later, as she was pulling into a parking slot of her garage, she saw Chris standing by the elevator. Just seeing him had her heart feeling lighter than it had all day.

''Good evening, Congresswoman.'' He stood aside as she stepped into the elevator.

She glanced at the huge cardboard box in his hands. ''Pizza?''

''You bet. Tony makes the finest.''

"You wouldn't mind giving me a sample on the way up, would you?"

"Not a chance." At her floor he followed her out of the elevator and started along the hall. "First you're getting out of that proper business uniform and into something more suitable for pizza and beer."

She touched a hand to her heart. "Pizza and beer. Who'd have believed such words could make my poor heart flutter?"

Laughing, she fished the key out of her pocket and opened the door of her apartment. Chris followed her inside and headed straight toward the small kitchen. By the time she'd changed into casual knit slacks and a matching top in lemon yellow, the room was filled with the fragrance of Italian spices. The table was set for two, and two frosty mugs of beer sat side by side on the countertop.

"Oh, Chris." Bren picked up a mug and drank. "This was worth coming home to."

"So is the sight of you." He gave her a long, appraising look, from the bare toes peeking out beneath the cuffs of her slacks, to the cap of red curls that looked pleasantly disheveled. Then he picked up a mug of beer and touched the rim to hers. "Here's to unwinding after a long day at the office."

"Umm." She sipped, then turned toward the pizza. "Can we eat now? Or are you going to torture me by making me wait?"

"We'll eat." He set out two salads and a basket of breadsticks, then carried the steaming pizza to the table.

As Bren set to work on the food, he watched with a growing smile. "Tell me something. If I hadn't come along to feed you tonight, what would you be eating right now?"

She thought a minute. "I have a couple of frozen dinners in the freezer. When I'm really desperate, I'll heat one up. But usually I just have tea and toast with peanut butter."

He was shaking his head. "If the voters heard that, what would they think?"

She laughed. "I'm sure they'd be really disappointed. They probably think that everyone who works in Washington goes to banquets and black-tie events every night in the week."

He set a second slice of pizza on her plate before helping himself to another. "Speaking of black-tie events, there's a police charity event coming up this weekend. I was hoping you'd go with me."

She looked up. "You want *me* to go to a police event?"

He nodded.

"I don't think that would be wise, Chris."

"Because you think it's a conflict of interest?"

She shook her head. "Because I'd feel as welcome as an ant at a picnic."

He laughed. "Hey. Ants have to eat, too."

"If they live long enough. Sometimes they get squashed."

"Nobody's going to squash you, Congresswoman." He closed a hand over hers, sending a flood of heat along her arm. "I'll be right beside you the entire evening."

"Great." She pulled her hand away. "You'll protect me and ruin your own reputation in the process."

"Is that why you're refusing? To spare my reputation?"

She studied him across the table. "Chris, in case you haven't noticed, my committee is investigating your officers. And there isn't a single member of the force who isn't aware of that fact by now. I'm sure they'd make their feelings abundantly clear, not only to me, but to you, as well. They wouldn't be too happy with the man who brought an enemy into their camp.''

He leaned back. ''You see what's happening here? A line's being drawn in the sand. Instead of working together to root out the problems that are giving cops a bad name, we're taking sides. The public is beginning to think all cops are corrupt. And the force itself is closing ranks, trying to pretend that there are no problems at all, except in the minds of some politicians.''

''I wish you had said that today on the news, instead of suggesting that this whole thing had been invented by someone looking for his fifteen minutes of fame.''

''I said a whole lot more. But the only thing that sticks in your mind is that one phrase.'' He grinned. ''It seems to me we've gone down this road before.''

Bren flushed. ''Sorry. I ought to know better than anyone how our words can be twisted when taken out of context.'' She sat back, leaving her third piece of pizza half-eaten. ''I surrender. If I eat one more bite, I'll explode.''

''How about some coffee?''

She started to get up, but Chris touched a

hand to her shoulder and crossed to the counter, filling two cups.

Bren sipped, then sighed. "You're spoiling me, you know."

"Good. That's my intention."

She looked over at him. "You do realize that your remarks on television today gained you a few enemies. My colleagues will be gunning for you."

"The way mine are gunning for you?" He surprised her by setting down his empty cup and reaching for her hand. "Come on."

"Where?"

"To that sofa in the other room."

"Why?"

"I can see that you're not ready to give up this debate just yet. And as long as we're going to debate issues, we should at least do it where we can be comfortable."

As Bren sank down on one end of the sofa, she watched Chris kick off his shoes before sitting down on the other end and stretching out his long legs in front of him.

"Why don't you go first, Congresswoman."

She grinned. "You're trying to soften me up. First that food, and now a comfortable place to sit. But this is serious business, Chris. Your department can't stick its head in the sand and keep pretending there isn't a problem within its ranks. Innocent citizens have been killed.''

He nodded. ''And all the evidence points to a rogue cop. Or maybe a couple of them. The latest autopsy is in.''

Bren sat up straighter. ''What did it prove?''

''That the bullet came, not from a police-issue gun, but from a gun that was supposedly in the police property room.''

''Oh, Chris.'' She wasn't even aware that she'd brought her fingers to her temples to rub at the tension building there. ''You see, that just proves what I...'' She swallowed back the rest of whatever she'd been about to say as he slid closer and turned her slightly before lifting his hands to her temples.

''What are you...?''

''Shh.'' He began to massage gently. ''I can see that you need this.''

''I don't need—''

''Quiet, Congresswoman. I told you. I do my best debating while I'm rubbing my opponent's back, or feet, or...other parts of the anatomy.''

''I suggest you keep your hands on my head at the moment, Captain.''

''Yes, ma'am.'' But as he continued his gentle massage, he could feel her beginning to relax. ''There, now, doesn't that feel better?''

''Mmm. Much.''

He brought his mouth to her ear. ''Now about that autopsy.''

She shivered as his warm breath tickled. ''What autopsy?''

He laughed, sending a series of tremors along her spine. ''Now, this is what I call a serious debate.''

''Not fair.'' She turned to face him, but he surprised her by lifting her feet to his lap.

As he began rubbing she burst into a spasm of giggles. ''Stop. Chris. That tickles.''

''Just relax. I'm an expert at this.''

She closed her eyes as he continued his gentle ministrations until she found herself actually beginning to relax and drift on a cloud of contentment. He had the most amazing hands. With each stroke she found herself sinking deeper and deeper.

''Now, Congresswoman, if there's any point

you'd care to make, you have my complete attention.''

"You don't play fair." She opened her eyes and found him studying her with a wolfish look that had her heart racing. "You know I can't think when you're rubbing my feet."

"All part of my devious plan. So, do you concede this round to me?"

"Maybe." She couldn't help sighing just a little. "Next time I'll just have to figure out how to take advantage of you the same way, so the playing field is level."

"You want to know how to take advantage, Bren?" He released her feet and slid closer. "Just keep doing what you're doing."

"I'm not doing anything except arguing with you."

"That's just it." He framed her face with his big hands. "I love your quick mind, and your tart tongue, and those wise turquoise eyes. In fact, Congresswoman, I think everything about you is sexy as hell." His look was practically devouring her. "And if I don't get out of here right this minute, I just might forget my manners and seduce you."

He kissed the tip of her nose before getting to his feet and heading for the door.

She struggled off the sofa and followed him. As he started out the door she called, "Will I see you tomorrow?"

He paused a moment, as though waging a battle within himself. Then on a moan he turned back and dragged her into his arms.

It wasn't the kiss that startled her; it was the barely controlled passion. Just moments earlier he'd been laughing with her, teasing her, kissing the tip of her nose. But this was no playful romp. This had all the ferocity of a tornado, hurling her into something for which she was totally unprepared.

The hands gripping her upper arms were almost painful as he drove her back against the wall, his hard body imprinting itself on hers, while his mouth, that firm, clever mouth, plundered, until she was dazed and breathless. And still he continued, spinning the kiss on and on until, with a moan, she was forced to clutch his waist or risk falling bonelessly to the floor.

When at last he lifted his head, they both stood perfectly still, struggling to drag air into their starving lungs.

He stepped back. "Wild horses couldn't keep me away from you, woman. Now don't forget to set that alarm."

"I...won't." She was amazed at how difficult it was to get even those words out. Her throat was dry as dust, and her heart was pumping furiously, as though she'd been running for miles.

She stared at the closed door for long minutes. When she was finally able to move, she threw the bolt and punched in the code. Then she crossed her arms over her chest and leaned weakly against the door, wondering what in the world had just happened.

She felt as though she'd just been tossed into a storm and had somehow lost all sense of direction.

Chris Banning was either the best thing that had happened in her life lately or the worst. Either way, he was definitely becoming a problem. One she would rather not have to deal with at the moment.

Chapter 6

"I hope you haven't forgotten our date, Congresswoman."

At the sound of that deep voice on the other end of the telephone, Bren had to struggle to stay focused. She'd been immersed in a committee report, and suddenly she found herself remembering, for at least the hundredth time, that devastating kiss. "Date?"

"A black-tie affair. You do own a formal, I assume."

"One or two."

"Good. I'd advise you to wear only one of them. I'll pick you up at seven."

She couldn't help laughing. "Are you sure you want to do this?"

"Absolutely. Don't try to wiggle out of it. Got to run."

She replaced the receiver, then closed her eyes for a moment. It looked like one more night when she wouldn't have time to read the committee reports that were assuming the thickness of a dictionary.

As she returned her attention to her daunting schedule, it occurred to her that scant years ago she'd have spent the entire day preparing for a black-tie affair by pampering herself. She would have gone into a panic if she couldn't find time for a manicure and fancy hairdo. Since joining the ranks of Congress, she simply hoped for five minutes to put on makeup and slip into her gown.

She stuffed documents into her attaché case and started toward her first meeting of the day. And though she was able to stay focused on the business at hand, every once in a while she found herself thinking about Chris Banning in a tuxedo. The thought never failed to bring a smile to her lips.

"Well, Captain Banning." Bren couldn't help staring as she opened the door to her apartment that evening. The image she'd carried in her mind all day couldn't hold a candle to the real thing. "You look so distinguished."

"And you look—" he gave her a long, admiring glance that had the blood rushing to her cheeks "—absolutely amazing. Who ever said redheads shouldn't wear red? That's a dynamite gown."

Laughing, she twirled. "You like it?"

He studied the slim column of red silk, with its thin spaghetti straps, scoop neckline and narrow skirt that brushed the tips of matching red strappy sandals. It managed to be both sophisticated and sexy as sin.

He touched a fingertip to her cheek. "Are you sure you're Bren? Or did she hire some gorgeous movie star to stand in for her?"

Laughing, she caught up a small red evening bag and folded a fringed shawl over her arm.

When she turned, Chris brought one hand from behind his back and held out a nosegay of white roses.

Caught by surprise, she ducked her head and breathed in their fragrance. But not before he saw the look of pleasure in her eyes.

"I wasn't expecting this, Chris. They're beautiful."

"They don't even come close to you. I figured white was safe, since I didn't know what color you'd be wearing." He offered his arm. "Come on. You'll get to listen to a bunch of boring speeches after they allow you to enjoy your dinner."

"That's all right." She linked her arm with his. "It's a small price to pay for the chance to see you in a tuxedo."

"You think so?"

She nodded as they headed toward the elevator.

Inside he shot her a sideways glance. "Then just wait until you see me out of it."

Their laughter continued as he linked his fingers with hers and led her toward his waiting car.

As he drove through the streets of the city, Bren turned to him. "I still think you're making a mistake bringing me tonight. There are going to be plenty of your friends on the force who won't be pleased."

"That's their problem."

"But you have to work with them, get along with them, long after this is over."

He glanced at her. "And your point is?"

"They could make your life miserable."

He merely grinned. "Bren, my life was miserable for years. Nothing they could say or do could even come close to what I've already been through. Now relax." He closed a hand over hers. "If you play your cards right, you may even get me onto the dance floor."

"You dance?"

"Not well. But at least I won't step all over your feet."

"That's good. In these shoes, that could be a disaster."

As they drove up to the hotel, a valet took their car. Chris hurried around to open Bren's door and take her arm. When they stepped into the ballroom, they were met by a sea of men in tuxedos and women in gaily-colored gowns, with waiters threading their way through the crowd, balancing trays of drinks.

"Here you are, Chris."

A white-haired man clapped a hand on Chris's shoulder.

"Chief. A good-looking crowd." Chris dropped an arm around Bren's shoulders. "I'd like you to meet Mary Brendan Lassiter. Bren, this is Chief Roger Martin."

"Chief Martin."

"Congresswoman." The chief arched a brow. "I didn't know you and Chris were friends."

She smiled. "We met at a taping of *Meet the Media.*"

With a straight face Chris added, "I have you to thank for that, Chief."

"So you do." The chief's lips curved with laughter. "I watched that show. The two of you did equally fine jobs. I thought at the time that you were well suited to the debate at hand. But I never dreamed you'd carry on the debate afterward. That is what you're doing together, isn't it?"

Chris grinned. "You might call it that."

"Enjoy yourself, Congresswoman Lassiter." The chief gave her a warm smile before turning away to greet another couple.

"Hey, Captain." A handsome young man paused beside Chris. "I've never seen you at one of these charity events before."

"I've never had the desire to attend before now. Trevor Sinclair, I'd like you to meet Bren Lassiter."

The young man gave Bren a long, lazy appraisal before extending his hand. "Congresswoman. I believe your grandfather knew my grandfather, Travis Sinclair. ''

Bren searched her mind, then shook her head. ''I'm afraid I don't recall the name.''

He merely smiled. ''They served on the force together years ago.'' He looked beyond her to Chris. ''You always had good taste, Captain.''

Before he could say more several more couples pushed between them, and Trevor Sinclair was lost in the crowd.

''Come on. I think you've had your ego stroked enough for now.'' Chris caught Bren's hand and began leading her through the crowd searching for their table. ''First we need to find a place to sit. Then I'll get us both a drink.''

When they located their table, Chris gave their order to a waiter, who returned within minutes with their drinks.

As Chris introduced Bren to the couples at their table, she couldn't help noticing their various reactions as recognition dawned on them.

''You're the congresswoman whose committee wants to bring in outside investigators?'' Noah Swale, the burly man seated to her right, didn't bother to hide his anger.

Bren met his narrowed look. "Our committee has made no recommendations as yet. We're still considering a dozen or more options.''

"I love your dress,'' the man's wife said, to smooth over the awkward moment.

Bren smiled at her. "Thank you.''

"You'll need a helmet and body armor if this crowd recognizes you,'' Noah said under his breath.

Bren kept her smile in place. "I guess I'll be safe enough here, with all these brave officers in the room.''

His head swiveled to meet her look. "I wouldn't count on it, Congresswoman.''

Before he could say more his wife led him away from the table, while several other couples looked on with growing discomfort. But from the smug looks on a few of the faces, it was obvious that there were many who agreed with him.

When the music began playing, Chris pushed back his chair and took her hand in his. "Dance with me, Bren.''

Once on the floor they moved together

slowly. Against her temple Chris muttered, "Sorry about that. Noah's a good cop. But he's always been a hothead."

"There's no need to apologize, Chris. You can't control what others say or do."

He looked down at her. "You handled it well."

She shrugged. "Goes with the territory."

"Yeah. The cool congresswoman. Don't forget, I've seen you face down an attacker's gun, Bren. I know what kind of courage burns inside you."

"There are different degrees of courage. That night I had no choice but to stand up to the gunman. At the moment I'm feeling very much like an object of curiosity. The proverbial fish out of water."

He glanced around and realized that heads were turning as they danced by. "I hadn't noticed. But since they're already watching, let's give them something to talk about." He drew her even closer, pressing his lips to her temple while he executed a series of smooth turns.

She held on, enjoying the way they moved as one. "You really can dance."

"Only when I have an inspiring partner." When the music ended, he continued holding her while he murmured, "What I'd like to do is get out of here right this minute, so we could do some dancing in private."

She looked up and found his mouth hovering mere inches from hers. She could feel the heat pouring between them. "Are you sure dancing is all you have in mind?"

"What I have in mind..." He looked up suddenly as someone bumped him so hard he was shoved against Bren.

If he hadn't had his arms around her, she would have gone flying into a table at the edge of the dance floor.

He turned with a frown to find Trevor Sinclair in a shoving match with Noah Swale. The two men glared at each other and lifted their fists, before being subdued by others in the crowd. Minutes later the meal service began, and the incident was forgotten.

"I see what you mean about a hothead," Bren muttered. "Or do all cops just have hotter blood than mere mortals?"

"We're definitely hot-blooded." As he led Bren to their table Chris leaned close to whisper, "This meal won't be as good as Tony's, but I'm told the prime rib isn't bad."

"You seem to be always feeding me."

He held her chair and pressed his mouth to her ear. "Yeah. It's a tough job, but somebody has to do it."

Bren watched warily as Noah Swale started toward their table. It occurred to her that his last name could have been whale. Even a tuxedo couldn't camouflage the protruding stomach. Before he'd taken half a dozen steps his wife caught his arm and steered him toward the bar. Everyone at the table seemed relieved.

Bren bit into her prime rib and sighed with pure pleasure. "Now this is worth a dozen long-winded speeches."

Chris chuckled. "You say that now, but once they start, you'll be as bored as the rest of us."

Half an hour later a gavel was pounded and the speeches began, honoring several members of the force who had gone through the community raising money for the charity in question.

Bren saw the pride on the faces of those officers who were singled out by their friends and colleagues. Each name brought thunderous applause. Their acceptance speeches were brief and humble.

She leaned close to Chris. "You were wrong. These aren't at all boring."

He merely grinned. "I wasn't talking about these. Wait until we get to the real speech-makers. They could even out-talk your committee members."

"That would take some doing."

He winked. "Trust me."

An hour later the awards portion of the ceremony was over, and the speeches began in earnest. Speeches on behalf of the police department. On behalf of the charity that was to benefit from the evening's event.

When the last speech ended and the crowd began mingling, Chris caught Bren's hand, and the two of them slipped away.

At the door she paused. "Are you sure you should leave? Won't your chief expect you to stay and mingle?"

"He'll never even miss me." He handed his receipt to the valet.

While they waited for his car, they stood together under the canopy. When Bren shivered, Chris took the shawl from her hands and draped it around her shoulders, allowing his hands to linger a moment. Just then his car came to a screeching halt. He helped Bren into the passenger seat, then hurried around to the other side.

As he drove away he lifted his hand in a salute.

Bren turned to see Trèvor Sinclair standing at the curb. She made a mental note to mention him to her grandfather.

She leaned her head back and closed her eyes as the car sped along the darkened street.

Chris looked over. "Tired?"

"A little." She turned toward him, admiring his handsome profile. "You?"

He shook his head. "I could have danced all night."

"Funny. You didn't seem all that eager to go on dancing while we were at the party."

"I prefer to do my dancing in private."

"I see."

"Of course," he deadpanned as he pulled into her parking garage. "some people might not call what I do dancing." He walked around and held her door, then linked fingers as he led her to the elevator.

"Really?" She looked over at him as the numbers flashed by over the door. "What do they call it?"

"It's known by many names. But the moves

are pretty much the same." He walked beside her until they paused outside her door.

She fished out her key, and he opened the door. Bren deactivated the alarm, then turned to him in the doorway.

The look in his eyes had her heart racing.

He lifted a hand to her shoulder. "Would you like me to show you?"

"Show me what?"

"Some of my moves."

"I think I've had enough dancing for to-night."

"That's a shame." He ran a finger around the dip in her neckline and watched the way her eyes seemed to glow with fire as his fin-gertip brushed the soft swell of her breast.

Her heart was doing more than race now. It was actually vibrating loudly enough in her ears that she was certain he could hear.

She took a step back, breaking contact. "Thanks for feeding me, Chris."

"And the dancing?"

"Very nice. Maybe we'll do it again some time."

"Oh, we will, Bren. Count on it." He seemed to consider for a moment, then turned and stepped out of her apartment.

"Wait." She took a step toward him and touched a hand to his arm. Just a touch, but she felt the way he seemed to stiffen. "Would you like to come in? I could make coffee."

"No coffee." His tone sounded unusually gruff. "No joking now. If I come back in, I won't make it out until morning." He paused. "Your call."

"I see." She swallowed, then lowered her hand to her side. "Good night then, Chris."

"Good night, Bren." He turned away. Over his shoulder he called, "Sweet dreams."

She listened to his retreating footsteps before bolting the door and activating the alarm.

Sweet dreams? She doubted she'd even be able to sleep tonight, let alone dream. But she would, she knew, be replaying every word, every touch, for the rest of this night.

Chapter 7

"Congresswoman Lassiter."

Bren looked around in surprise at the number of reporters and photographers charging toward her. Because there was no way of escaping with her dignity intact, she put on a smile and faced them.

"About the results of the autopsy," one reporter shouted. "Are you surprised?"

"I'm disappointed to learn that the bullet came from a gun that was stolen from the police property room. But I'm sure the department will take the necessary steps to find the one who committed this terrible crime against an innocent citizen.''

''This wasn't just another innocent victim,'' a television reporter shouted above the din. ''This was a whistle blower. Someone who had publicly criticized the police force for its lax security within the police department. Do you agree with the *Washington Dispatch* that this latest murder appears to be part of a conspiracy?''

Conspiracy. The very word sent ice along Bren's spine.

She held up a hand. ''I'm sorry. I must confess that I haven't read the *Dispatch*'s report. When I've had time to go over it, I'd be more than happy to get back with you.''

''Congresswoman Lassiter.'' A reporter from the *Dispatch* barred her way, while his photographer snapped a dozen or more shots in quick succession. ''Are you saying that you and the other members of your committee aren't aware of the depth of corruption within the police department?'' He held up a copy of the morning edition of his newspaper, which had begun its own investigation. ''And that you haven't read about the latest scandal?''

He saw her eyes widen at the headline,

while his photographer snapped off yet another shot.

"Our reporters have uncovered the fact that
more than one hundred kilos of cocaine have
disappeared from the police property room
over the past year."

"They may have been misplaced..."

He shook his head. "It was only after the
Dispatch began our investigation that police
discovered the cocaine in the bags had been
replaced by flour. This was no accident. This
was a deliberate act, carefully planned and executed by someone within the department who
knew about the lax security and felt confident
it would never be discovered."

Bren managed to maintain her composure,
though it was an effort. "As I said, I haven't
had a chance to read the report. When my
committee has all the facts, a statement will
be forthcoming."

"What do you say to those rogue cops out
there who are committing these crimes?"

She struggled to control her sense of outrage. "The brave men and women who put
their lives on the line each day shouldn't have
to see their department sullied by such low-
lifes." She stared directly into the camera.

"To those of you committing these despicable crimes, be warned. Your days are numbered."

She pushed through the crowd, aware that the cameras continued to record her every movement. Though she wanted to run, she forced herself to walk slowly up the steps until she was able to slip through the doors. With a nod to the morning guard, she hurried along the halls, eager to hide inside her own office.

Once there, Juana Sanchez was waiting, with a stack of newspapers already on her desk.

Her assistant looked up as she passed. "You read the latest?"

Bren shook her head. "Not yet. But I got a preview from the hordes of reporters waiting out there on the Capitol steps."

"You usually catch the news before you get to the office."

Bren nodded wearily as she let herself into her inner office. She slumped down at her desk and opened the first newspaper, reading quickly before moving on to another and then another. All carried basically the same information, although the report in the *Dispatch* was the most detailed.

If the rumors were to be believed, a rogue

cop, or perhaps a group of them, had decided to take the law into their own hands. Not only were they targeting anyone who criticized the department, but they had now moved on to stealing from their own. Drugs. Money. Guns. All taken from the police property room. If it hadn't been for the investigation by the *Dispatch,* the thefts might have gone on indefinitely.

Bren sat back, sipping the coffee Juana had placed on her desk and berating herself for having been caught off guard by the press. She couldn't recall a morning when she hadn't taken the time to read half a dozen newspapers while monitoring several news shows, and all before she was even showered and dressed. But today had been different. She'd spent half the night tossing and turning, unable to sleep. This morning she'd been only half-awake while she pulled herself together for work. And all because of Chris Banning and the way he'd taken over her emotions.

She couldn't recall a man ever affecting her this way before.

There had been plenty of men in her life. But she'd never known anyone like Chris. He was a maze of contradictions. So smooth and polished, as though he'd spent a lifetime with tutors and prep schools. All cool and controlled, whether facing an armed attacker or the slings and arrows of the media. But she was beginning to see another side to him. A side that excited her even while it frightened her.

What did she really know about Chris Banning? Could he be using her for his own purposes? Could he have decided to cozy up to her in order to keep her committee at bay until his own department could clean up their act?

She was feeling suddenly very unsure of herself. And completely vulnerable. And she knew why. She was losing her heart to this man. And she wasn't at all sure whether or not he returned those feelings.

This could all be just a game to Chris. The thrill of the chase. The lure of another conquest. But once he caught her, he could be the type of man to simply walk away and search for the next challenge.

"Bren." Juana hurried into her office, closing the door behind her and leaning on it as though guarding it with her life. "Congressman Roland Paxton is here. With blood in his eyes."

Bren took in a breath, then slowly exhaled and pretended to draw a sword. "Okay, Juana. Turn the lion loose."

"Bren." Juana poked her head in the door. "Your grandfather's on line two."

Bren snatched up the receiver. "Hi, Pop."

"The whole gang's coming tonight for dinner, lass. Can you make it?"

Just hearing that brogue had the tension easing from her shoulders. "I'd love to. I may be a little late, but keep a spot for me at the table."

"That's my girl." The old man's pleasure could be heard in his voice as he rang off.

Bren tackled her paperwork with a vengeance, determined to work her way through as much as possible before heading to her mother's house. She wasn't, she told herself firmly, taking refuge here in her office to avoid the reporters. But after having her hide almost ripped off by Roland Paxton, she'd nursed her wounds by closeting herself at her desk for the remainder of the day.

She'd read all she could on the *Dispatch's* in-depth investigation of police corruption. It appeared, at least in the view of the newspaper's reporters, to be much more deeply entrenched than first suspected. Though none of the force had been willing to go on the record, several had suggested that the damage had been limited to one or two highly placed officers. All who had been interviewed had expressed outrage over the damage being done to the reputation of the entire police force.

Was it possible for all of this to go on without the knowledge of the men at the top? What about Chris? He was the youngest officer ever to attain the rank of captain. It was said that he was one of the most popular officers on the force. Would he compromise his integrity for popularity?

There it was again. That tiny fear nibbling at the edges of her consciousness. Now that it had been planted, she couldn't seem to ignore it. In a fit of anger she swept a pile of documents from her desk, watching as they drifted to the floor. Then, annoyed at her reaction and humbled by the thoughts she was entertaining, she got down on her hands and knees and began picking them up and stuffing them into her briefcase.

Minutes later she stepped out of her office.

"Juana, I'm leaving for the day. If you need me, I'll be at my mother's."

"I'm glad to hear it. You've been putting in way too many hours." The older woman noted the bulging briefcase. "You should leave that here and deal with it tomorrow."

"Not a chance." Bren managed a wry laugh. "If the reporters are waiting to pounce on me again in the morning, at least I won't be caught with nothing to say."

"You did just fine." Juana ignored the ringing phone long enough to add, "I watched your segment of the news. I was proud of you."

Bren blew her a kiss as she sailed out of the office without waiting to see who was calling. Tomorrow was soon enough to deal with the phone messages. Right now she was going to relax and forget about everything except sharing a few laughs with her family.

The Beltway traffic had long ago dissipated. As Bren headed home she felt her heart soar at the familiar sight of the Washington Monument towering over the graceful landscape. She loved this city. And though she often felt overwhelmed at the amount of work she'd undertaken, she loved her job, as well. It was frustrating at times, trying to please both her constituents and her fellow congressmen. But she'd known going into the job that it wouldn't always be smooth sailing. She'd always loved a challenge. And now that she'd had a chance to bounce thoughts and ideas off her levelheaded family for the evening, she was feeling once more in control.

There wasn't anything she couldn't do if she set her mind to it. And right now she'd decided that she would get to the bottom of this police corruption scandal, and let the chips fall where they may.

As she pulled into the parking garage of the Middlegate Apartments she experienced that odd tingling along her spine and berated herself for her weakness. She couldn't go on cringing every time she came home late at night. Still, she fished her cell phone out of her bag before getting out of the car. Tossing her purse over her shoulder she grabbed up her briefcase and headed for the elevator.

All the way up she felt uneasy. When the doors slid silently open, she glanced around before stepping out at her floor. As she started along the hallway she could feel the hair at the back of her neck begin to rise. Twice she paused and, seeing no one, continued on. Long before she reached her door she had the key in her hand. She unlocked her door and stepped inside, relieved to be home at last. But when she lifted a hand to the alarm pad, she realized that it had been turned off.

Had she forgotten to set it this morning? She'd been distracted over thoughts of Chris. Still, she hadn't been that distracted. She distinctly remembered setting the alarm.

Her hand was shaking as she punched in a phone number on her cell phone.

She could hear Chris's voice, thick with sleep. "Banning here."

"Chris."

When he heard her fear, his tone sharpened. "Bren? Where are you?"

"I just got home. Someone's been here. My alarm was turned off."

"Get out of there. Dial 911 and lock yourself in your car. I'll be right over."

"All right. I—" She was about to run from her apartment when she saw something red scrawled on her bedroom door. "Wait. What's this?"

* * *

Chris was shouting at her through the phone while he struggled into his clothes and snatched up his weapon from a drawer beside his bed. "What do you see? What is it?"

"There are words. Scrawled on my bedroom door. I think they're—" she paused "—written in my lipstick."

"Bren." His tone was frantic now. "Don't stay. Don't read what it says. Just get out of there."

She wasn't listening. Aloud she read, "'This is what happens to meddlers.'" She shrugged. "That's all it says. But there's an arrow pointing to the doorknob."

"Bren." Chris headed out the door of his apartment and ran toward his car. "Don't break this connection. Do you hear me? Just stay on the line. And whatever you do, don't open that bedroom door."

"But I—"

He swore violently as he turned the key in the ignition and began racing through the darkened streets of the city. "Just this once, don't argue with me. Just hang on, and I'll be there in a couple of minutes."

He was as good as his word, leaving his car

parked beside hers at the Middlegate Apartments and taking the stairs at a run rather than wait for the elevator.

With gun in hand he kicked in her apartment door and glanced around the empty room. His first thought was that she'd been abducted. Then he realized that the door to her bedroom was standing open.

He walked past the message written in bold letters in blood-red lipstick.

"This is what happens to meddlers."

Inside he was relieved to see Bren staring wordlessly at her dresser. The mirror above it had been shattered. Glass littered her dresser top and the floor around it.

He waited just a moment, until he felt his heartbeat begin to settle. Then he holstered his gun and went to her, wrapping his arms around her waist, drawing her back against him.

"Are you okay, baby?"

At the sound of his voice she swallowed, then nodded, still too overcome to speak.

He pressed his face into her hair. "You can't stay here."

She took a deep breath. "I have to. Don't you see?"

"No, you—"

She pushed free of his arms and turned to face him. "I can't let someone run me out of my own space."

Her face was deathly pale. So pale it frightened him. But he could already see the fire of anger in her eyes. "All right, then. I'll bring in a team of police..."

She stiffened and backed away. "I don't want them here."

His eyes narrowed. "You've already got them here. Like it or not, I'm one of them, Bren."

"I know." She clasped her hands, then unclasped them. "I can't believe I called you. I have a brother in the security business. Another who has more connections in Washington than the president. Yet I called you." She shook her head, as though trying to fathom what she'd done.

He took a step closer and touched a hand to her shoulder. "You called me because you know in your heart I'd never let anything happen to you."

She looked up, meeting his eyes. After several long moments of silence she nodded. "You're right. Until this moment, I wasn't sure. But now..." She let out a long, slow breath. "Thank you for coming, Chris. I was so scared."

"So was I, baby." He drew her into the circle of his arms and allowed himself to breathe deeply. Against her temple he whispered, "Oh, God, you'll never know how much."

Chapter 8

"Come on." Chris kept his arm around her shoulders as he steered her toward the kitchen. Once there he urged her into a chair. "What'll it be? Coffee? Or your grandfather's Irish whiskey?"

"I think I'd like the whiskey." Bren could feel the reaction setting in. She felt suddenly cold and weak and light-headed. She glanced toward the bedroom door, where the lipstick-smeared words mocked her.

Seeing the direction of her gaze, Chris filled two tumblers with whiskey and sat down across from her. When she arched a brow, he gave a weak grin. "Last time I only had to face an armed coke-head. This time I had to face my fears for you all the way here. You'll never know how many things I imagined." He drained his glass in one long swallow.

Bren took a sip and felt the whiskey burn a path of fire down her throat. Then she shakily got to her feet. "I'd better start cleaning up that glass."

He stood and closed a hand over her arm. "Sorry, Bren. Not yet."

She shot him a look.

"Like it or not, this is a crime scene. And that means that I need a team of professionals to go over it." When she started to protest he merely sighed. "I know you don't know who to trust right now. But you've admitted that you trust me. Right?"

She nodded.

"And I intend to handpick men and women that I trust." He drew her close and began rubbing his hands up and down her arms. She was so cold. He could feel her shivering with each touch. "If the intruder left even one small clue, Bren, I want it. And the only way to find it is to let my people go over your apartment with a fine-tooth comb. I promise you, they'll be every bit as concerned about your safety as I am.''

As much as she wanted to resist, she wanted even more to feel safe again. To be free of this fear. "I guess, if you think it's right..."

"I do."

She gave a slight nod of her head. "All right. I'm too tired to argue."

"That's my girl." He kissed the tip of her nose as he reached for his cell phone.

A short time later he said, "You'll need to pack some things."

She looked at him blankly.

"My team will be here most of the night going over your apartment. I think it's best if you pack enough clothes for tomorrow and sleep elsewhere."

"And where would you suggest I sleep?"

"I was thinking about my place—" he gave her one of those devilish smiles that always stopped her heart "—said the spider to the fly."

"I hope you understand this is only for one night." Bren wearily followed Chris through the door of his tenth-floor apartment.

They'd waited more than an hour for his

team to arrive and begin the tedious task of sifting through every shard of glass, every thread on the floor, countertop and piece of furniture. Once the professionals had gotten started, and had given Bren their word that this latest incident wouldn't become public knowledge, Chris had led her to his car for the ride across town to his place.

She glanced around as he began turning on lights. It was a purely masculine space. Deep-green carpeting, with caramel-colored leather sofa and green-plaid armchair and ottoman. Two walls of the great room were lined with bookshelves. Tucked between rows of books were framed awards. She walked closer to study them. One for marksman. Another for officer of the year. On one shelf was a framed photo of a much younger Chris with an older man and woman, all smiling for the camera.

She looked up and saw him watching her. ''What did you do with the Bannings' house?''

''Sold it.''

''Why?''

He shrugged. ''It was time to move on with my life. And this was closer to my work.''

She glanced around. ''This is nice.''

"Thanks."

She motioned to the exercise machines that took up the other half of the room. "Can't the department afford a gym?"

He laughed. "We have a really great gym."

"Then why all this?"

He shrugged. "On nights when a particularly tough case keeps me awake, I like to work out until I'm tired enough to fall asleep."

He touched a button, lighting the gas fireplace. Within minutes warmth flooded the room while the flames flickered silently.

He crossed to the door and picked up her overnight bag. "You can have the bedroom."

"Where will you sleep?"

Again that wolfish smile. "If you're going to be selfish and keep the bed all to yourself, I'll have to sleep on the sofa. But if you're feeling generous..."

She took the bag from his hands and stepped into the bedroom. "Enjoy the sofa, Captain Banning. You can have that cozy fireplace all to yourself."

"I was afraid of that."

He watched as the door closed. He waited until the count of ten before knocking.

Bren crossed to the door and opened it. She'd already removed her suit jacket and had kicked off her shoes. She eyed him suspiciously.

"I'll need my stuff." He stepped into the bedroom and sauntered to the adjoining bathroom, wishing he'd given her just a little more time. Another ten or twenty seconds and she'd have been out of that skirt and blouse, as well. The thought of it had him sweating.

After retrieving his shaving kit he paused at the door. "I'm afraid we'll have to share the shower in the morning, since the other room has only a half bath. But because you're my guest, I'll let you go first, as long as you promise not to hog all the hot water."

"Generous of you." She smiled as she closed the door in his face. A moment later he heard her turn the lock.

"Hey." He rapped a fist on the door. "What if I need something else?"

"I guess you'll have to do without."

"There's a definite mean streak in you, Congresswoman."

"That's what my brothers always said."

He was grinning as he strolled across the room and began undressing. Dropping down to the edge of the sofa, he picked up his cell phone and dialed. Moments later he kept his voice low as he said, "Banning here. How's it going? Any clues?"

He listened, sighed, then said, "Call me when you're done there. And remember—I don't care how unimportant it may seem. I want anything at all that seems out of place."

He set aside the phone and lay back, folding his hands under his head, watching the play of moonlight on the ceiling. It was bad enough knowing that someone in his department had gone outside the law. He'd known, since it had first become apparent, that it was only a matter of time until the rogue cop was caught. But now time had become a critical factor. Unless this nutcase was caught quickly, he could strike again. He'd made no secret of the fact that Bren was his next target.

Or was she?

Chris got to his feet and made his way to the first exercise machine, a step climber, working it until his legs ached from the effort. All the while he mulled over his latest question.

Why had Bren been given this warning? If someone had wanted her dead, it would have

been an easy matter to stand just inside her
door and wait for her return. The alarm had
already been disconnected. A quick hit, and
the killer could have walked away without a
trace. Instead, he'd scrawled words on a door,
and smashed her mirror. As frightening as that
might be, it wasn't fatal. It was merely meant
to frighten, leaving her a fighting chance.

Was that what this was all about? Was the
killer really looking for a fight?

But what chance did a public figure like
Bren, who'd made no secret of her distaste for
guns, have against an armed intruder? Unless,
of course, it wasn't just Bren who was the in-
tended victim.

Chris thought about the black-tie dinner. It
had been easy to spot the angry reactions of
some of his colleagues. Not all the anger had
been directed at the congresswoman who was
investigating their department. Some of it had
been aimed at him, for bringing the enemy
through the gates. And then there was that first
night when he'd been waiting at Bren's door.
She'd come barreling into him, scared out of
her wits because she'd sensed that she was
being followed.

If she had been followed, and if that person

had spotted him at her door, the connection had been made. The black-tie dinner would have sealed that connection. Anyone wanting to hurt one of them could easily decide that the best way to do that was to hurt the other.

Chris made his way to the rowing machine and settled himself. As his arms strained against the tension of the oars, he realized it was all beginning to make sense. If someone had a grudge against him, what better way to hurt him than to hurt the woman who had suddenly begun to mean so much to him? He'd made no secret of his feelings. He paused to pass a hand over the sweat that rolled into his eyes. And he'd foolishly paraded her in front of everyone in the department at the awards banquet.

He muttered a vicious oath. He'd unwittingly tossed her into a tank filled with sharks. Now it was up to him to save her. He had to figure out who would want them both dead.

He got to his feet and returned to the sofa, rolling into the blanket as he vowed to do whatever it took. Until this was over, his only mission was to keep Bren safe. If he failed that, his own life would mean nothing.

* * *

In the bedroom, Bren lay in the big bed,
breathing in the scent of Chris that lingered in
the bed linens. There was something so calming about his presence. Something so fierce
and protective about him, that gave her a sense
of safety. Still, even knowing he was just outside her door, she felt alone and vulnerable.

She could hear the hum of the exercise machines, and knew that Chris had found his own
way to work off his frustrations.

She closed her eyes, willing herself to sleep.
But sleep was impossible. All she could see in
her mind's eye was the door of her room and
the lipstick-red words scrawled across it. With
that image came the return of the sheer terror
she'd experienced when she'd found her mirror shattered.

It gave her such an eerie feeling to know
that a stranger had violated her space. Had deactivated her alarm system. Had walked
through her rooms. Had freely gone through
drawers and cupboards, touching her personal
belongings.

She hugged her arms around herself, feeling
her skin crawl at the thought.

And then another thought intruded. She

could have walked in on the stranger while he was there. She thought of the attack in her parking garage. Were the two related? The police had assured her that her attacker was still behind bars, awaiting trial. Did he have a friend? A family member, seeking revenge? But if so, why hadn't he waited behind her door until she'd returned? After all, there was a rogue cop, or several of them, terrorizing citizens. And she had, as the spokesman for her congressional committee, turned up the heat. It seemed reasonable to assume that she would be on the top of a hit list. But she hadn't been killed; merely warned. Maybe it was being done to make her squirm. A little fun, perhaps, before the final blow?

She shivered, knowing she was in over her head. She didn't have the street smarts for this kind of thing. In the morning she would phone her brother Micah and tell him what was happening. As a former member of the Secret Service, he had access to the most highly qualified bodyguards in the business. She would ask him to assign one to her until this madman was found.

She could have asked Chris to take her to her mother's place tonight. But she hated putting her mother and grandfather through this again. They were still on pins and needles about the first attack. A second one would have them watching her like a two-year-old toddler heading toward a cliff.

She punched a fist into the pillow and rolled to her side, determined to sleep. But though she spent another hour with her eyes tightly closed, her mind refused to shut down. At last she gave up and tossed aside the covers. Shoving hair from her eyes, she paced to the window, where she drew open the blind to peer at the lights of the city spread out below.

She hated feeling afraid. It was so alien to her. She thought back to the time when she'd lost her father. Though she'd been brokenhearted at her loss, she hadn't been afraid. Especially after her father had sat beside her on her bed looking just as he always had. So big and strong and handsome, with that wonderful glint of humor that always danced in his eyes.

Know this, Mary Brendan. I'll always be here for you, just as I've been since the day you were born. Do you believe that?

She had. And though she hadn't given it much thought lately, she still believed.

She hugged her arms around herself and

whispered, "Oh, Dad. What a mess. I don't want Mom and Pop worrying themselves sick over me. But I know the minute I phone Micah, he'll tell them everything."

She walked back to the bed and sank down on the edge of the mattress. Almost at once she felt a presence beside her, and a thought came to her in a sudden flash of insight. The man in the next room would gladly lay down his life to keep her safe. There was no one better to have beside her than Chris Banning.

Bren stood and began to pace the floor. What had happened to all her doubts? Suddenly they'd been swept away so completely, it was as if they'd never existed in the first place.

She pressed her fingertips to her temples, wishing Chris were here to rub away her headache. But she could tell, from the silence in the next room, that he'd finally worked off his frustrations and had gone to sleep.

She sighed as she experienced a sudden craving for a soothing cup of tea. She opened the door and crept toward the kitchen, using the light from the fireplace as a guide. As she passed the sofa she had to fight an almost-overpowering desire to wake Chris and throw herself into his arms. Instead she moved resolutely to the kitchen. Once there she quietly closed the door and switched on the light before making her way to the sink.

It took only a minute to fill a kettle with water and turn on the stove. While waiting for the water to boil she rummaged through the cupboards until she located a package of tea.

She was just turning toward the stove when the door opened.

"Chris." She looked like a kid with her hand in the cookie jar. "I'm sorry. I was trying to be so quiet. Did I wake you?"

He flashed her that heart-stopping grin. "Please. Don't apologize, Congresswoman. Especially since I finally get to see what you wear to bed."

Chapter 9

Chris studied the blue-and-white, man-tailored nightshirt buttoned all the way to her chin. It might have been prim except for the fact that the shirttail barely covered the essentials.

"Great legs, Lassiter."

"Thanks." She couldn't deny the shiver that passed through her at the way he looked, barefoot and naked to the waist, his jeans unsnapped as though he'd pulled them on in haste. He was thoroughly rumpled, his cheeks and chin darkened by stubble, his eyes bloodshot from lack of sleep. He looked dark and dangerous and incredibly sexy.

"Your backside's not bad, either, Bren." He craned his neck. "You wearing anything under that shirt?"

"I might ask the same about those jeans."

"I'll show mine if you'll show yours."

"Guys." She shook her head and reached for the kettle.

"If you're making tea, make two cups."

He reached over her head and removed a second cup and saucer, then continued standing right beside her while she poured the water over the tea bags.

"You smell good." He bent close to breathe her in, and she felt a sudden shock to her system.

She turned with a frown. "You know exactly what you're doing, don't you?"

He looked offended. "And what would that be?"

She handed him a cup. "Pushing me. To see how far I'll let you go."

"Really? Tell me, Congresswoman. How'm I doing?"

"You're good. But you forget. I have three

brothers. That makes me well aware of how guys operate.''

''Oh, yeah. I know how smart you are. And how tough.''

''That's right.'' She gave him a smug look. ''Now that we have that settled…''

''It's far from settled.'' He set down his cup and took hers out of her hands.

She shot him a puzzled look. ''What're you…?''

He backed her against the counter and unbuttoned the top button of her nightshirt. ''No more lines. No more games or tricks.'' The laughter was gone from his eyes. In its place was a dark, smoldering look that had her heart beating overtime. ''I want you, Bren. I've never wanted anyone or anything as badly as I want you.''

She put a hand to his chest to hold him back.

He stunned her by lifting it to his mouth. ''I've been lying on the sofa for the past hour thinking I'd have to break down my own door just to get to you. And then, wonder of wonders, the door opened and out floated this angel. You made it all so easy. Now here we are, and it's time for some honesty.''

"Chris, this isn't smart."

"Maybe it's the dumbest thing we'll ever do. I don't care about smart or dumb. I just know I've been half in love with you since the first time I saw you, standing there facing that madman and waiting to die."

She felt his words wash over her and wondered at the thrill that shot straight to her heart.

He brushed his mouth over hers, tempting himself with the taste of her, the sweetness of her. And all the while his hands moved up and down her arms, sending sparks dancing across her flesh.

"I'd like to do the noble thing, the honorable thing, and tell you to go back to my bedroom and lock the door. But it's too late for that now, Bren. The way I'm feeling, there isn't a lock anywhere in this place that could keep me from you."

He lifted his hands to the second button of her nightshirt, all the while staring deeply into her eyes. "There's one thing that can stop me. And only one."

He paused and saw her arch a brow.

"Just tell me to stop, Bren. If you do, I may go half-mad with the feelings threatening to explode inside, but I'll stop."

Without a word she went very still, and he felt his heart skip a beat. Then, just as misery was turning into despair, she stood on tiptoe to reach his mouth. As she did, she moved aside his hands and unbuttoned the second button, then the third, until her shirt parted.

She heard him suck in a breath as his gaze moved over her. Then with a sly grin he touched his hands to the silk ties at either side of her hips. "Such naughty panties, Congresswoman. Do you suppose if I pull this tie…" He smiled as the pale blue bikini pants parted and drifted to the floor. With a growl of pleasure he dragged her into his arms. "You do know how to torture a man."

"It's not something I was planning. I still can't believe this is happening."

"Me, neither. Though I can't say I haven't been planning this since the night we met." He brought his hands to her shoulders, sliding the nightshirt down her arms. "I'm just glad we both lost our senses together." He trailed soft moist kisses down the smooth column of her throat and heard her suck in a breath of pleasure. The sound had all the blood rushing to his loins.

Her skin was as soft as the underside of a

rose petal. In fact, she smelled like roses. The scent filled his lungs as he feasted.

Helpless to do more than whimper in pleasure, she let her head fall back, giving him easier access. As his eager mouth moved lower, she had to remind herself to breathe in and out.

His hands, those big, clever hands, were moving over her, causing the most amazing heat to build deep inside. Deliciously weak, she gripped blindly at his waist, needing to anchor herself. The touch of his naked flesh had her fingers tingling. She brought her hands slowly up, palms flat against his chest, and felt his breath hitch.

The thought of taking her here, now, had his heart thundering. It was what he wanted. What they both wanted. Still, he forced himself to take in a long, deep breath and slow down. Though he knew he would soon have to end this madness, he wanted so much more.

He pressed his mouth to a tangle of hair at her temple. "Do you know how many ways I want to love you?"

"Tell me."

His grin was quick and deadly. "I'd rather show you."

In one smooth motion he scooped her up and headed out of the kitchen. He was hoping to make it to the bedroom, but after only a couple of steps he had to pause to taste her lips once more.

That was his undoing. The minute his mouth was on hers, he felt the room begin to tilt and whirl. Dizzy with need, he veered toward the sofa. But when she tangled her hands in his hair and moaned with pleasure, he stopped dead in his tracks, taking the kiss deeper.

She fumbled with the snaps at his waist and heard his guttural curse as he kicked aside his jeans. She looked down, then began chuckling. "Why Captain Banning. No underwear?"

"No time. Come here, woman." He hauled her into his arms and kissed her until they were both breathless.

He couldn't get enough of her. With every kiss, every touch, he wanted to crawl inside her skin. To take and give until they were both sated.

As the kisses became more demanding, he felt the heat rise up between them, threatening to choke them. He thought about making it as far as the sofa, but even that was too much effort. Instead he lay with her on the rug, feeding from her mouth like a man starved for the taste of her.

"I thought I could wait, Bren." His eyes looked hot and fierce in the glow of the fire. His body glistened, all damp muscles and sweaty flesh. "But I have to have you now."

There was something so wild, so primitive about him. She felt herself being drawn down into the darkness of those piercing eyes. Into the desperate desire of his tortured soul. It was deeply arousing.

With a sigh she tangled herself around him, hot flesh to hot flesh. He shocked her by pulling back and raining kisses down the length of her body until she was trembling with need.

When he brought her to the first climax, she was so stunned she could do nothing more than cry out his name. She was still reeling when he took her again. Higher. Faster. And then again.

Each time she thought he would surely end this, he found another way to shock her until, sobbing his name, she clutched at him and nearly begged.

He was beyond hearing. Beyond seeing. His heart was rocketing so loudly in his chest, he wondered that it didn't simply explode. Half-blind with need, he wrapped himself around her as he entered her.

In that same instant, she opened to him and took him in fully.

For the space of a single heartbeat they paused, staring deeply into each other's eyes. They were all they saw as they came together in a deep, searing kiss.

Then they were moving, climbing, soaring, before shuddering and falling slowly back to earth.

"You okay?" Chris didn't move. Couldn't. The thought of moving away from her was too painful to contemplate. If he could, he would stay just here, just like this, wrapped around her forever.

"I'm fine." Her voice sounded faraway even to her own ears.

"Yeah." He brushed his mouth over hers. "You're more than fine, Lassiter. You're—" he shook his head "—amazing."

"You're not bad yourself, Banning."

"Not bad?" He looked down at her with that cool, self-assured grin. "Admit it, Congresswoman. That was fantastic."

"It was...all right."

"Liar." He rubbed his lips over hers. "Tell me you didn't see stars."

"Oh. The stars." She couldn't help laughing at the frown line furrowing his brow. She touched a finger to the spot. "All right. That may be a first for me. I don't believe I've ever seen stars before."

"That's better." He smiled.

"Maybe it would have been better if you'd found us a soft bed instead of this hard floor."

"You call this hard?" He rolled aside and lifted her on top of him, cushioning her body with his. "Now, woman, this is what you call hard."

That had her bursting into spasms of laughter. "There's that male vanity again."

"Oh. I see. You think I'm just bragging?" He ran his hands lightly down her back, causing her to wiggle.

Suddenly she went very still. Her eyes widened slightly. There was no denying the fact that he was fully aroused.

He tangled his fingers in her hair and brought her face down until their lips met. Against her mouth he muttered, "I don't know about you, but I'm ready for more."

"Yes." With her body already highly sensitized, she wrapped her arms around him and sighed as they came together again. "Oh, yes."

They had no need for words as they took each other on a long, slow journey of desire.

"Mmm." Bren's nose wrinkled slightly at the wonderful aroma of fresh coffee. She poked her head up from beneath the covers to glance around. It took her a moment to remember where she was.

Sometime in the night Chris had carried her to his bed, where they had giggled like children and rolled around in an orgy of lovemaking that had left them, instead of exhausted, so charged with energy, they'd been unable to do more than doze.

He set down two mugs of coffee and crawled into bed beside her. "I figured since we never got that cup of tea last night, I had a solemn duty to make you coffee."

"It smells wonderful." She sat up, shoving hair from her eyes, and accepted the mug from his hand. After one sip she sighed. "Oh, it's heavenly. Thanks."

He set a plate between them. "I toasted a bagel."

She pried it apart. "What? No cream cheese?"

He grinned. "I make you coffee and a bagel at dawn, and all you think about is what I forgot."

"You don't like cream cheese?"

"I love it. But I don't happen to have any."

"Well, if you want me to bunk here again, you'll have to remember to buy some."

"I'll put that on my to-do list."

She bit into the bagel and made a little purring sound as she chewed. "This is wonderful. Want some?"

She held it out and he took a bite.

"I thought for a minute you were going to hog the whole thing."

"I did think about it." She laughed. "That's what comes of living with three brothers. I learned to zealously guard my food." She offered him another bite, then polished off the last crumbs before sipping her coffee.

He saw her looking around. "What do you need?"

"I need to know what time it is. I thought I spotted a clock earlier tonight."

"You did. I hid it."

She shot him an amused look. "You hid it? Why?"

"So neither of us would know what time it is."

"I don't understand."

"I figured our time together was too special to be wasted wondering if it was time to get ready for work."

"So you hid the clock?" She was laughing as she shook her head. "Did you think we could just forget about our obligations and stay here all day, playing in bed?"

"Yeah. I did." He trailed a finger along her arm to her shoulder, then down past her collarbone to her breast, where he slowly circled, all the while watching her eyes. "Have I told you how much I love your freckles? Like this one." He pressed his mouth to one at her collarbone, then began following a trail of freckles to her breast.

"Chris." She nearly bobbled the mug before setting it aside.

"Smart move, Congresswoman. What I'm about to do to you calls for both your hands to be free of hot coffee or sharp objects."

She was giggling as he tugged her down into the covers.

"Hmmm. I seem to have found more interesting freckles."

Minutes later her laughter turned into a moan of pleasure as he took her on a slow, delicious ride to paradise.

The ringing of the phone woke them. Bren shoved red tangles from her eyes as Chris grabbed the phone on the second ring.

"Banning."

He sat up on the edge of the bed, suddenly alert. "You're sure?" He listened a minute longer before saying, "I can't be there this morning. But maybe this afternoon."

Fishing through her things on the night table, Bren found her watch and gave a gasp. It was already after nine. She had a committee meeting at ten. With a last glance at Chris, still talking on the phone, she made her way to the bathroom and brushed her teeth before turning on the shower.

She'd just stepped inside and lathered her hair when she heard the door open.

"I'll be through here in a minute," she called, ducking her head under the spray.

Chris wrapped his arms around her, drawing her firmly against him as he pressed his lips to the back of her neck.

"Chris." She sighed as he continued kissing her while his clever hands began to work their magic.

"This was another one of my fantasies when we first met." He turned her into his arms and lifted her.

"All right. Now I know you're crazy."

"Like a fox. Are you saying you'd rather take a pass, Congresswoman?"

In answer, she brought her mouth to his.

As the warm spray played over them, they gave themselves up to the madness of the moment.

Chapter 10

"Juana?" Bren held the phone to her ear while balancing on one foot and slipping the other into a shoe. "I'm running late. Would you phone my committee members and ask if they could convene their meeting in our offices? That way I ought to be able to make it in time. Thanks."

She dropped the phone and leaned on the dresser top to slip on the other shoe. When she looked up, she could see her reflection in the mirror, and behind her, Chris as he walked up and closed his arms around her waist, his thumbs resting just beneath the fullness of her breasts.

"Do you have any idea how incredibly sexy you are, Congresswoman Lassiter?"

She gave a throaty laugh. "No. Why don't you tell me?"

He pressed his mouth to her cheek. "I love seeing you all buttoned up in a proper business suit." He burned a trail of kisses to the corner of her mouth. "It really turns me on to hear you talking to your assistant about committee meetings."

She brought her hands over his. "Then you ought to see me signing documents."

"Be still my heart." He pressed a kiss to the hair at her temple.

"Or maybe you'd care to hear me present my views on the disposal of industrial waste to the House chairman next week."

"I wouldn't be able to restrain myself. I'd have to ravage you in the House chambers."

"There are laws against that, Captain Banning."

"I'd throw myself on the mercy of the court. Any man seeing you would understand my lack of control. In fact, I believe I feel a lack of control coming on right now." He

turned her and pressed her back against the
dresser as he gave her a lazy, heart-stopping
kiss.

"Oh, Chris." She sighed, then pushed free.
"Do you have any idea what time it is? I have
a meeting to chair."

As she started to pick up her purse, he
hauled her into his arms again and kissed her
until she could feel the room start to spin.
When he lifted his head she experienced a moment of complete disorientation. She could
swear the room was still moving.

He was grinning at the look on her face.
"Come on. You'll be late."

"For what? Oh yeah. I remember. Work.
Committee meetings. Congress."

He handed her the purse that had fallen to
the floor, then caught her hand and led her to
the door. "Just remind me where we left off
when we get back here tonight."

She held back. "I thought I'd be going back
to my apartment after work."

"You will." He set his security alarm, then
closed and locked the door. Dropping an arm
around her shoulders he walked with her to
the elevator. "But first we'll stop by here so
I can pick up a few things."

"Why?"

"Because." He stepped into the elevator and punched the button, before drawing her close. "You don't think I'm going to leave you alone in your apartment, do you?"

She felt the warmth of his words wrapping around her heart. In truth, she'd been uneasy about returning alone to her own place.

Seeing the flicker of emotion in her eyes, he cleared his throat. "I need to say this, Bren. For years now I've been living just for the day. The moment. But right now, if I could give you security and peace of mind and the promise that you'd be safe tomorrow, I'd give it, no matter what the cost."

"Thank you, Chris."

He caught her roughly by the shoulders. "For now, all I can give you is my promise that I'll do everything in my power to stay by your side and see you through this."

She sighed and touched a hand to his cheek in a gesture so achingly sweet, he wanted to devour her. "How could I ask anything else of you, Chris? Just knowing you're beside me is all the comfort I need."

As the door opened, they stepped apart and made their way to his car in the parking garage. When they arrived at the Congressional Building, Bren was surprised to see Chris step out of his car and fall into step beside her.

"You don't need to go inside with me."

He merely smiled and took her arm. "I guess you weren't listening, Bren. I'm seeing you to your door."

At the door to her office she paused. "All right. You've done your duty, Captain."

He opened the door and followed her inside.

Juana Sanchez looked up from her littered desktop. "Good morning, Congresswoman." She looked beyond her to the handsome man in the police uniform.

Seeing her arch look Bren said, "Juana Sanchez, this is Captain Chris Banning."

"Captain. It's nice to meet you."

He crossed to her desk and offered a firm handshake. "Nice to meet you, Ms. Sanchez."

He turned to Bren. "I'd appreciate it if you'd stay inside until I come back to pick you up."

"Stay here? All day?"

He nodded.

Knowing Juana was listening, she frowned. "I'm not sure I can promise that. Things come up. And when they do, I can't just lock myself away in my office."

"Yes, you can. Do it, Bren. Just this once."

She sighed. "I suppose…"

"Good girl." He squeezed her arm. "I'll be here to pick you up by five o'clock."

"But I…"

With a smile at Juana, he breezed out of the office.

When the door closed, Juana picked up a sheaf of papers and pretended to fan herself. "That is one hot-looking man. Isn't he the one who appeared with you on *Meet the Media?*"

"Yeah. The same." Bren motioned toward her office door. "Is the committee meeting here?"

Juana nodded. "They'll be here at eleven. Stop trying to change the subject. How did your police captain happen to be here with you? And why are you, the most punctual person in this building, arriving more than an hour late? What have the two of you been up to?"

"I have work to do." Bren turned away and headed toward her inner office, leaving Juana staring after her with a knowing smile.

* * *

"Captain Banning's here to see you," Juana announced.

Bren looked up from the papers on her desk, astounded that the day had passed in a blur of work.

When Chris ambled into her inner office, she was stuffing documents into her briefcase.

"Good evening, Congresswoman." He closed the door firmly and leaned against it while crossing his arms over his chest. "How did your day go?"

"The better question would be where did it go. I can't believe it's after five."

"Is it that late?" He dragged her into his arms and kissed her soundly.

She pushed against him. "Chris. Someone could come in and see us."

"Sorry. This can't wait." He kissed her again, lingering over her mouth. "I told you I love the way you look all prim and buttoned up. Of course, I loved the way you looked last night, too, wearing nothing but a smile."

"You're terrible." She was laughing as she said it.

"And you're gorgeous." He took the heavy briefcase from her hand and held the door.

In the outer office Juana was busy on the

telephone when Bren and Chris called good-bye. She waved and continued talking as their footsteps receded along the hallway.

At the door to the parking garage Bren stopped to chat a moment with the security guard before following Chris to his car.

When they arrived at his apartment build-ing, Chris turned off the ignition. "I'll only be a couple of minutes. Then if you'd like, we can stop for dinner on the way to your place."

She nodded. "I'd better go up with you and make sure I packed everything. I was a lit-tle...preoccupied this morning."

"Yeah." He held her door and dropped an arm around her shoulders. "I like seeing you...preoccupied." He led the way inside the elevator and punched in his floor. "Maybe we'll try that again tonight."

"What makes you think I'll let you?"

He tugged on a lock of her hair. "You're easy, Lassiter."

They were still laughing as they stepped off the elevator and walked to his door. He turned the key and opened the door, then punched in his security code and led the way inside.

Bren walked to the bedroom and began

checking her overnight bag. She looked up to see Chris standing in the doorway scowling.

"What's wrong?"

"My security's been breached."

She was shaking her head. "I saw you turn off the alarm."

He nodded. "Yeah. He was clever enough to reset it before leaving. But someone's been here."

"How can you tell?"

"We'll talk when we leave here." He picked up her bag and took her arm.

Once more he set the alarm and turned the lock before striding toward the elevator. Minutes later they were roaring down the highway.

Bren could feel tension vibrating through him. "Tell me how you know someone was in your apartment."

"I'm a cop, Bren. I never take my security for granted. Especially right now. So I set a couple of traps, hoping to catch our rat. I didn't catch him, but he did manage to set one off." He turned to glance at her. "Now I need to take you someplace where he can't find you. Tell me how to get to your mother's place."

Bren was already shaking her head. "I can't go there. Mom will have a fit when she finds out what's been happening. And Pop. Can you imagine how mad he'll be if he hears about a second attack? Chris, they're still reeling from the first time. I can't do this to them again."

"You've got no choice. Now do you tell me how to get there, or do I phone a friend at City Hall?"

Bren huffed out a breath. "You play dirty, Banning."

"So does our rat. He's left me no choice but to play by his rules. Tell me where to turn."

She gave a wry smile. "You'll be lucky if I don't tell you where to get off."

He closed a hand over hers. "Think of me as your mother, reminding you that this is for your own good."

She shot him a sideways glance. "Funny. You don't look like my mother."

At Bren's directions, Chris turned into the driveway of a stately older house in Chevy Chase. He noted that several cars were already parked ahead of his. Judging by the frown on

Bren's face, she'd seen them, too, and wasn't happy about it.

"Family?" He rounded the car and opened her door.

"Yeah. That one belongs to my brother Micah. That one is Donovan's. And that lovely little sporty model belongs to Cam. Looks like the only one not here yet is my mother."

Just as she said that, a bright-red convertible pulled in behind them, and a woman stepped out who looked like Bren's twin.

"Mary Brendan." The woman raced up the driveway and caught Bren in a hug. "Oh, what a lovely surprise."

"For me, too, Mom." Bren turned. "Kate Lassiter, this is Chris Banning."

Kate accepted his handshake. "I saw you on *Meet the Media.* You handled your end of the debate very well, Captain."

"Thank you. I was so dazzled by your daughter, I wasn't sure just what I was saying. And now that I've met her mother, I see where she got her looks."

Kate beamed as she led the way up the steps. Before she could open the door it was yanked open and a handsome, white-haired man stepped out to catch Bren in a bear hug.

"Well, lass, it's about time you came home. Your timing couldn't be better. Now the whole family is here."

When she'd kissed his weathered cheek, Bren took a step back. "Pop, this is Chris Banning. Chris, my grandfather, Kieran Lassiter."

"Banning, is it?" The old man gave him a measuring glance as he offered his hand. "Nice to meet you, Captain."

"It's Chris, Mr. Lassiter."

Kieran laughed. "And I'm called Pop. Or Kieran. Mr. Lassiter was my father."

"Right, sir." Chris looked up to a sea of faces crowding around the front door. The three men were as tall as Kieran, with those same deep-blue eyes and dark, Irish good looks. After introductions, he began to sort them out.

The oldest, Micah, had his arm around the shoulders of his wife, Pru. Donovan was holding a little girl named Taylor in his arms. His wife, Andi, stood beside a boy of perhaps eight, named Cory. Cameron, the youngest of the Lassiter men, was being teased about his latest girlfriend—a joke he wasn't taking with much grace. It was, apparently, a sore spot for him.

"Come in," Kieran urged, holding the door. "No sense standing out here all night. I have a fine pot roast cooking, along with all the trimmings."

Kate had her arm around her daughter's waist, and the two women led the others through the great room, past the dining room, to what Chris assumed was the heart of the house—the kitchen. There, while he stood and watched in wonder, everyone seemed to have a chore.

Micah was opening a bottle of red wine, to celebrate the arrival of his sister, though Chris assumed they would have found something to celebrate even without Bren's presence here.

Kieran was stirring something on the stove. Pru stood beside the old man, chatting easily. Donovan handed his little girl a basket of rolls, while his son was assigned the chore of pouring milk from a pitcher into two tall glasses, before carrying them to the dining room.

Bren left her mother to cross the room. "Feeling a little lost?"

He nodded. "How can this many people work in one room without stepping on each other's toes?"

"Oh, a few toes do get stepped on from

time to time. But the Lassiters always manage to get over it.''

Micah offered his sister a glass of wine, then handed one to Chris. ''So. You're a D.C. cop.''

Chris nodded.

''So was our dad.''

''So I've heard. His name is still a legend in the department.''

That had Kate touching a hand to Kieran's arm. The two shared a look before returning to their chores.

Kieran sliced the roast beef and arranged it on a platter. ''You're young to be a captain.''

Chris grinned at Bren. ''I worked hard.''

''I'll bet you did. But you had to have more than hard work going for you. Awards?''

Chris shrugged. ''A few.''

''More than a few, I'd wager.'' Kieran picked up the platter. ''Come on. Dinner's ready.'' He looked over at Kate. ''And for the first time in weeks all our chicks have come home to roost at one time.''

Chapter 11

Chris watched as the Lassiter family gathered around the table and joined hands. When Bren's hand found his, he gave her a look that practically devoured her, causing heat to flood her cheeks.

"Bless this food." Kieran intoned. "And this family. Not only those of us gathered here, but those who are here in spirit, especially Riordan, who watches over us all."

At the intensity of the old man's words, Chris felt a shiver along his spine. What must it be like to be so beloved as to become immortal? That's what had happened in this family. It occurred to Chris that this old man, and his beautiful daughter-in-law, had seen to it that Riordan Lassiter lived on in the minds of his entire family, decades after his death.

He accepted a platter of beef from Bren and helped himself before passing it on to little Taylor. When she had trouble holding it, Chris gave her a gentle smile. "Here. I'll hold it while you take what you want."

"Thank you," she whispered shyly.

"Have you sorted us all out yet?" Across the table Cameron was busy passing the potatoes.

"I'm trying." Chris took a roll and handed the basket to Bren.

"Micah's the oldest. He was in Secret Service. Now he has his own private security company. Why Pru was crazy enough to marry him is anybody's guess." For that remark Cam got a playful smack on the arm from his sister-in-law.

He pointed with his fork. "Donovan won't talk about his government service, which is fine with us because it was probably pretty boring, anyway." That brought a round of laughter. "Now that he's an old married man, he and Andi and the kids live in the hills of

Maryland while he finishes a book about international criminals.''

"Really?" Chris arched a brow. "Sounds fascinating.''

Cameron shook his head. "Even without the uniform, we'd know you're a cop. Only another cop would be interested in the criminal mind.''

That had everyone laughing louder.

"What about you, Cameron?" Chris glanced at Bren's youngest brother. "You don't look like a cop to me.''

"Lawyer," Cam said matter-of-factly. "I work at Stern, Hayes, Wheatley.''

Chris looked suitably impressed. "Good firm. Probably the best in D.C. You must be good.''

Bren laughed. "You shouldn't have stroked his ego. Now he'll never get that head through the doorway.''

That had the entire family roaring.

"Especially," Micah added, "since Cam uses that pickup line on all the women he wants to impress at Flannery's.''

"You have to admit that it works." Cam helped himself to more salad. "I'll have you know that the girl being ogled by the entire saloon last night left on my arm.''

''Probably because she was too drunk to stand by herself.''

That remark from Donovan had them laughing and hooting.

''See the abuse I take?'' Cam sipped his tea and winked at Taylor, who was laughing along with the adults.

Bren touched a napkin to her mouth. ''I guess I'll have to do the bragging about Mom, since she's too humble to talk about herself. She went back to law school after Dad passed away and is now a family advocate.''

''Pretty impressive,'' Chris said.

''And then there's Pop, who cooked and cleaned, washed and ironed, and kept us all together when we were falling apart.''

The old man smiled at his granddaughter. ''That went both ways, Mary Brendan. The lot of you kept this old man going when his world crashed and burned.''

Cory drained his glass of milk. ''Now that our adoption is final, I'm a Lassiter, too. And Dad says I'm going to be the strongest Lassiter of all.''

Chris turned to study the little boy. ''Re-

ally? That's pretty special. I was adopted,
too.''

Taylor and Cory sat up straighter, looking
at him with new respect.

''Did you have any brothers or sisters?''
Taylor asked shyly.

Chris fell silent.

Taylor glanced across the table. ''Aunt Pru
never had any brothers or sisters, either. But
she said if Uncle Micah hadn't asked her to
marry him, she'd have asked Pop to adopt her,
just so she could be part of the family.''

That had Chris choking back a laugh.
''Quite a tribute to this family, I'd say.''

''Or it explains why Pru was crazy enough
to marry my brother,'' Donovan deadpanned.

Kieran pushed away from the table. ''Now
you'll all stop picking on our Prudence.'' He
dropped a kiss on her cheek before saying, ''I
baked a cherry pie. Who wants theirs plain,
and who wants vanilla ice cream with it?''

''I'll give you a hand, Pop.'' Micah scraped
back his chair.

As he started toward the kitchen, Cam
called, ''He just wants to make sure he gets
the biggest piece.''

Micah chuckled. "You got that right, bro. I bet you're sorry you didn't volunteer first."

While they passed out the desserts, Kate poured tea. It was, Chris thought, so normal. And yet, in his entire life, he'd never experienced anything quite like the Lassiters. They seemed somehow bigger, funnier, louder than any family he'd ever known. An entire clan of overachievers. Yet there was so much love here, mixed in with the teasing banter.

He felt a hand on his and looked up to find Bren studying him.

"Where'd you go just now?"

He shrugged. "Just thinking how much I'm enjoying myself. You've got quite a family."

"Yeah." She looked around. "I do, don't I?"

They enjoyed their dessert and several cups of tea, before everyone began working together to clear the table. When the dishes were loaded in the dishwasher, and the pots and pans had all been scrubbed and put away, Cory and Taylor went out in the backyard to toss the basketball through the faded hoop hanging over the garage.

Kieran wiped down the kitchen counter and glanced at Bren and Chris, who were standing together, watching the children through the window.

When they turned, he arched a brow. "Something you wanted to tell us, Mary Brendan?"

"You could always read me, Pop." She cleared her throat and glanced at her mother. "I didn't want to worry you, but Chris insisted on bringing me here so I'd be safe."

The entire family went very still.

Kieran knotted the dishcloth in his hand. "Safe from what?"

"There was an...incident at my apartment."

The old man's eyes narrowed. "Don't stop now, lass. You have some explaining to do."

"Someone broke into my apartment and...wrote a message on my door before shattering my bedroom mirror."

Micah interrupted. "What did the message say?"

Bren turned to him. "It said this is what happens to meddlers."

His look was so intense, she could almost see the wheels turning in his mind. "And then you found the shattered mirror."

"Yes."

He glanced beyond her to Chris. "I'm sure you used your connections to see that it didn't make the news."

"So far. Bren and I both agree that we don't want to give this nutcase the publicity he so obviously craves. Of course, it could still be leaked to the press."

"Yeah. It could." Micah saw the frown on his grandfather's face. "So this happened yesterday?"

"The day before." The minute the words were out of her mouth Bren could feel her face flame.

"Why didn't you come home then, lass?" The look Kieran gave her was fierce.

"Because I didn't want all of you to worry the way I can see you worrying right now."

"Where did you go?" Cameron looked as intense as Micah.

"I went with Chris to his apartment."

Kieran's gaze narrowed on the man beside his granddaughter. "So why didn't you go back there tonight?"

"We did." Chris kept his tone level, hoping to downplay the danger as much as possible. "But I found the security in my apartment had been breached, and decided that Bren needed to get as far away from there as possible.''

''I'm glad one of you had some sense.'' Kieran wadded up the dishcloth and tossed it savagely into the sink. ''A family full of professionals, and you take your safety to a stranger.''

Kate laid a hand on his arm. ''I doubt that Bren considers Captain Banning a stranger, Kieran.'' She'd seen the looks exchanged between her daughter and this police captain. And though she ought to be more than ready to accept a man in her daughter's life, the truth was, she'd been caught completely by surprise. Still, she managed a smile. ''And Captain Banning is, after all, as professional as anyone in this room.''

Chris gave her a grateful smile. ''Thanks, Mrs. Lassiter.''

''I think you should call me Kate.'' She crossed the room and caught her daughter's hand. ''Why don't we go in the great room and you can give us a few more details.''

As Kate and Bren led the way, the others followed. But when Chris headed toward the door, Kieran stopped him with a hand on his shoulder.

Chris paused and looked over at the old man.

"You've some explaining to do, boyo."

"Explaining?"

Kieran saw his three grandsons turn back. With a look of annoyance he said, "We'll be along in a minute. I just have a few things to say to Captain Banning in private."

When they were alone he said, "You may not have noticed, but our Mary Brendan is a very special person."

"Yes, sir. I've noticed."

"Have you noticed, too, that her heart is a fine, fragile thing?"

At a loss for words, Chris merely nodded.

"Good. Now I'll remind you, Captain Banning, that if our Mary Brendan's heart should become shattered the way her mirror was, I'll hold you personally responsible. Is that understood?"

"It is."

"That's good, boyo." He dropped an arm around Chris's shoulders, and squeezed.

Despite the old man's age, Chris realized he had a grip like a steel vise.

Micah watched as his grandfather and Chris stepped into the great room. "I was just trying to convince Bren that she should let me assign her a bodyguard until this situation is resolved.''

Chris sat down on the arm of Bren's chair and placed a hand over hers. ''It's a good idea. I'd personally feel better, but I think your sister would feel it was too intrusive.''

''Yeah. That's what I'm hearing.'' Micah ran a hand through his hair in frustration. ''But intrusive is better than dead.''

That brought Kate out of her chair. ''Why can't she simply stay here until this madman is caught?''

''Because, Mom, I have this job.'' Bren looked around at her family. ''I can't hide indefinitely. There's no telling how long it will take to find this person. If at all. In the meantime, I have to continue representing my district in Congress. I have no intention of allowing this…threat to send me into hiding.''

''It seems to me,'' Donovan said quietly, ''that someone has gone to a lot of trouble to rock your world, Bren. Any idea who it might be?''

''My committee is looking into the use of excessive force by some police officers. One theory is that it could be a rogue cop, hoping to teach me a lesson in meddling.''

Donovan turned to Chris. ''Do you agree with that theory?''

Chris nodded. ''It seems reasonable to me.''

Kieran slapped a fist into his palm. ''In my day men wore their uniforms with pride.''

''Even in your day there were a few bad apples, Pop.'' Micah dropped an arm around his wife's shoulders. ''I seem to recall one or two officers who left an awards ceremony and helped themselves to a shop owner's profits on the way home.''

Kieran's eyes narrowed at the memory. ''I'd forgotten. For years afterward, that shop owner cringed every time he saw a man with a badge walk into his place of business. It's a shame that one or two troublemakers can give the entire force a bad name.''

Chris nodded. ''It's the same now. Because of a few, the rest of us are suspect.'' He turned to Micah. ''I really like the idea of a personal bodyguard for Bren.''

When she started to protest he merely smiled.

''So I've decided to pull rank and assign myself one special job. From now until this guy is caught and off the streets, you're not going to make a move without me beside you.''

She got to her feet, her hands on her hips. ''Haven't you been listening? I can't possibly function in Congress with a bodyguard getting in my way.''

''As I see it, you have two choices. You can hole up here in your mother's home until we get this guy. Or, if you insist upon continuing your very public life, you're going to find yourself stuck with me.'' His smile widened. ''Your call, Mary Brendan Lassiter.''

She slanted a narrow glance at her grandfather. ''He's beginning to sound suspiciously like someone I know. Did the two of you cook up this little plan in the kitchen?''

Kieran threw back his head and roared. ''I'm afraid not. But I do like the sound of it.'' He clapped a hand on Chris's shoulder. ''And I'm beginning to like you a whole lot more, as well, Captain Banning.''

''Thank you, sir. Then I take it you approve of my plan?''

''I do, indeed.'' The old man brushed a kiss over his granddaughter's cheek. ''I think you're going to be in very good hands, lass.''

"Men." She turned and stalked up the stairs. At the landing she called, "I'm sleeping in my old room. Someone can find a lumpy sofa for the arrogant police captain."

As soon as she was gone, Micah turned to Chris. "I think that may be the first time in the history of our family that the male of the species got the better of my bossy little sister." He gave him a high-five. "You have my admiration."

"And mine," Donovan said with a grin.

As the others gathered around, Kate watched with a look of puzzlement. Despite the fire in her daughter's eyes, she had the feeling that Bren wasn't nearly as angry about the arrangement as she let on.

Unless she was misreading things, her darling Bren wasn't just smitten. She was head over heels in love.

Chapter 12

Chris lay in the darkness, listening to the soft night sounds around him. Instead of the lumpy sofa Bren had recommended, he'd been given Micah's old room. The sheets were crisp and clean, the mattress firm enough for his big frame and soft enough to invite sleep. Yet here he was, hours after the others had gone to their beds, still tossing and turning.

This evening at Kate's had been enlightening. And certainly entertaining. He'd never known a family like this. No wonder Bren was comfortable working with men twice her age, wielding power with the best of them. She'd had an excellent training for the job with this bunch.

Riordan Lassiter was a legend among D.C. police. Though he'd been gone for more than twenty years, his reputation for heroism would never be forgotten in the annals of Washington lore. Maybe the younger members of the force would no longer recognize the name of his father, Kieran Lassiter, but Mike Banning had imbued in his adopted son a reverence for highly decorated cops, and Kieran had been one of them. It had been something of a shock to see a proud old lion like Kieran wearing an apron and doing kitchen duty. But after that first moment Chris had been able to look beyond the humble work to the man who still wielded power within his family. Kieran Lassiter was definitely the revered head of this family.

Then there was Kate, clearly the heart of it. She was still stunning. Not just physically beautiful, though her face was unlined and her eyes sparkled as brightly as Bren's. There was such inner peace and beauty about her. A woman completely content with her life. Not an easy accomplishment, considering that she'd been left to raise four children alone.

Her sons were something of legends themselves. Chris had heard of Micah Lassiter, and
had watched, along with the rest of Washington, as he'd taken a bullet meant for the president some years ago, ending his career with
the Secret Service. That scene had played on
news shows for days after the incident. It was
said that the private security company he had
founded employed only the toughest former
Secret Service agents, who were proud to
work for Micah Lassiter. Several times tonight
he'd seen Micah unconsciously rub a hand to
his shoulder. He'd be willing to bet a week's
pay that Micah still suffered twinges of pain
from that bullet wound.

Then there was Donovan. The way the family tiptoed around his government work, Chris
had a pretty good idea what it had been. There
was a feral look in his eyes that Chris had only
seen in the eyes of CIA veterans.

Cameron tried hard to play the role of party
animal. And with a paycheck from Stern,
Hayes, Wheatley he was definitely playing in
the big league. But Bren had said that her
brother also took pro bono cases from among
her mother's most desperate clients. Not all

heroes wore badges, Chris thought with a smile.

He shifted, wishing he could turn off his mind and grab some sleep. But no matter how he tried, he couldn't wish away the image of Bren as she'd flounced off to bed. He found that willful, independent streak in her incredibly sexy.

He wanted her. Desperately.

The thought of what they'd shared last night had him sweating. It was torture to know that, right now, this minute, she was sleeping just a room away.

He pounded a fist into the pillow and turned on his side. At least if he couldn't fall asleep, he could hope the night went by quickly. This was the last time Bren was going to be allowed to be out of his sight until they found their rogue cop.

Chris awoke to the most wonderful smells. Coffee, freshly ground. Cinnamon rolls baking in the oven.

He was already salivating when he slid out of bed.

There was a quick knock on his door, and

Kieran's muffled voice announced, "Your turn for the shower, boyo."

Chris was grinning as he made his way down the hallway. A few minutes under a hot spray had him fully awake. He wrapped a towel around his waist and started back toward Micah's bedroom. Halfway there a door opened, and he froze at the sight of Bren as she stepped from her room.

"Great suit, Lassiter. You'll wow them in the halls of Congress."

"Thanks." She had to swallow twice. The sight of him dressed in only a towel had her throat dry as dust. "I hope you're going to wear more than that. Having a bodyguard is bad enough. But having one wearing a toga will completely ruin my credibility."

"A toga, huh?" He moved in closer. "You smell great."

"So do you." She'd never before known mouthwash and shampoo to be so sexy. But then, maybe it had more to do with the man than the spicy fragrance. His face was clean shaven, inviting her touch. She curled her hand into a fist to resist. And those droplets of water glistening in his dark hair had her eager to run her fingers through the strands.

"You'd better hurry. Pop's breakfasts are important to him. He expects everyone to fuel their bodies for the coming day."

As she started past he stopped her with a hand on her arm. "You're all I need to fuel my body, Bren."

At the intensity of his words she closed her eyes, experiencing a tremor along her spine. She lifted a hand to his cheek. "I missed you last night."

He groaned. "Why didn't you let me know? I laid awake half the night wanting you."

Just then another door opened and Kate, dressed in a soft blue-gray business suit, stepped out. When she caught sight of them she paused for just a moment, seeing the way they stepped a little apart.

"Good morning." She turned to Chris. "I hope Micah's room was comfortable."

"Very comfortable. Thank you." He glanced down at himself. "I'd better dress. I'll see you both downstairs."

Bren and her mother watched as he hurried into Micah's room, closing the door. Then Kate tucked her arm through her daughter's as they descended the stairs. "It was grand having you back home for a night, darling. I only wish it were under cheerier circumstances."

"I'll be fine, Mom." Bren patted her mother's hand as they headed toward the kitchen.

"I know." Kate paused before opening the door. "You've always been very special to me, Bren."

Bren brushed her lips over her mother's cheek. "No more special than you are to me. You're one of my heroes, you know."

"Oh, you." Kate was almost blushing as she looked up to see Chris coming down the stairs.

The sight of his uniform gave her heart a little jolt.

He followed them into the kitchen, then stared around in surprise.

Cameron was grumbling as he piled bits of scrambled egg and crisp bacon bits onto a piece of toast, then covered it with a second piece, forming a sandwich.

"Not good enough, boyo." Kieran pointed his knife like a sword. "I'll not have you eating on the run. You can afford one more minute to sit at the table like a civilized man."

"These days, civilized men and women eat

in their cars, Pop. Haven't you heard of fast food?''

''Fast food.'' Kieran spat the words like expletives. ''It's neither fast nor is it real food. Tell me one of those burger places can make eggs taste like that.''

With a sigh Cam took a bite of his sandwich. Chewed. Swallowed. Then with a wink at his sister, settled himself at the big trestle table and took another bite. ''As always, Pop, you win. The only place I've ever enjoyed a Riordan sandwich is right here in my own kitchen.''

Chris poured himself a cup of coffee. ''What's a Riordan sandwich?''

''This.'' Cam pointed to his concoction. ''My dad always ate his scrambled eggs and bacon this way, stacked on a piece of toast, then covered by a second one. He always called it a Riordan sandwich.''

''Sounds good.'' Chris glanced at Bren, who was passing a platter of scrambled eggs across the table to her mother.

''Sit, boyo.'' Kieran turned from the stove. ''Nobody leaves my kitchen without eating breakfast.''

Chris laughed. ''You don't have to twist my

arm. It's been a long time since anyone other than the waitress at Tony's has cooked for me.''

"What about your mother?'' Kate looked up as he settled himself beside Bren.

"She's dead.''

"Oh, I'm sorry, Chris.'' She passed him the platter of eggs. ''And your father?''

"He's dead, too.''

Cam glanced over. ''You mean you have no family at all?''

"That's right.''

Chris could see, by the look on Cam's face, that he was having trouble imagining such a thing. Now that he'd met the Lassiter family, Chris could understand why. When surrounded by a brash, noisy herd, it must be next to impossible to picture a lone wolf. The thought had him smiling. Wasn't that how he'd always seen himself?

Beside him, Bren found herself thinking about Chris's birth parents. How tragic that they would never get to know the fine man who had completely transformed himself from the angry boy they'd deserted. They had failed him. Miserably. But they hadn't defeated him.

Like a phoenix he'd risen from the ashes of their misery.

"More coffee, lass?" Kieran hovered beside her chair.

"No, thanks, Pop." She shoved away from the table. "I really do have to get going. I have a committee meeting in less than an hour."

Chris drained his cup and followed her lead. He offered his hand to Kieran. "That was a great breakfast. And so was the dinner last night."

"Glad you enjoyed it, boyo." The old man gave him a long, level look. "You'll see to our lass?"

Chris met his eyes before nodding. "You know I will."

"One more thing, boyo." Kieran cleared his throat. "It was grand seeing a uniform in this house again. It's been such a long time and—" the old man shrugged, suddenly overcome "—I hadn't realized how much I'd missed it."

From her position by the door Bren saw her mother wipe a tear from her eye.

Kate scraped back her chair. "I hope the two of you are planning on staying here until this is resolved."

Chris glanced at Kate and saw her reluctant nod. "I was hoping you'd insist. As long as you don't mind the extra work, I think it's the wisest thing to do."

"Work?" Kieran scowled. "When it involves family, boyo, it isn't work. It's a labor of love."

Chris broke into a wide smile. "Then I guess we'll see you tonight." He followed Bren out the door.

When they were in his car, he turned the ignition before glancing over at her. "You were right."

"About what?"

"About your family. This has been quite an experience."

She laughed as he started along the quiet street. "You're just being polite. Admit it. Aren't you thinking that the Lassiters are a unique breed, unlike anything you've ever met before?"

He joined in her laughter. "You got that right."

As he turned into traffic he added, "You're lucky, Bren. We don't get to choose our families. But the one chosen for you is pretty special."

She fell silent, watching as he maneuvered through morning rush hour. She found herself wondering what her life would have been like if she'd been abandoned by the people she trusted and had had to fend for herself in a system that failed more often than it succeeded.

A sobering thought as she tried to mentally prepare herself for the coming day. Though she resented the thought of having Chris hovering around her, she couldn't deny that she found it comforting to know she wouldn't be alone.

Alone.

She glanced at Chris, seeing in that stern, chiseled profile, something she hadn't noticed before. Had she mistaken loneliness for anger? Did all that charm hide a lonely heart?

She pushed aside her thoughts and picked up her briefcase as Chris turned the car into a parking slot. She would need a clear head if she hoped to make a dent in the mountain of paperwork awaiting her in her office.

For once she was grateful for the work. There wouldn't be time to dwell on other things. Like a gunman, possibly a cop trained to kill, who could be stalking her this very minute.

Chapter 13

"There she is!"

"Wait, Congresswoman Lassiter."

As Bren started up the steps she was met by a sea of reporters and photographers, all vying for her attention.

"Congresswoman Lassiter, is it true that someone has targeted you for revenge?"

Caught by surprise, Bren looked over the faces of the men and women who had congregated so tightly around her it was impossible to move. For the space of a heartbeat she felt a rush of panic. Then, feeling a hand on her arm, she looked over to see Chris beside her, his steely gaze scanning the crowd.

His presence had a calming effect.

She took in a long, slow breath. "There was an incident, but I wasn't physically harmed. It appears that someone has gone to a lot of trouble to try to frighten me."

A microphone was thrust toward her. "Can you tell us what the incident was, Ms. Lassiter?"

"I'd rather not go into detail. As I said, I wasn't harmed."

"Do you think this is related to your committee's investigation of the police department?"

"I think this is related to the fact that I have a very high-profile job. I suppose it comes with the territory."

A reporter with patent-leather hair and a booming voice that could be heard above the din shouted, "What steps are you taking to protect yourself, Congresswoman?"

"You don't really think I'd reveal my strategy, do you, Russ?"

At her easy laughter, many in the crowd joined in.

"I see a police officer beside you," the man

shouted. "Are we to assume that he's been assigned for your protection?"

"You know better than to assume anything in this town, Russ." Seeing that she had won them over with humor she held up her hands for silence. "I'm awfully glad that you're all here this morning to help me get out the message that I will not be intimidated by threats. Now if you don't mind, I have a job to do."

Because they had their lead story, the crowd parted, allowing Bren to move smartly away. Chris kept pace beside her, all of his senses alert to the fact that any one of these people could be hiding a handgun. In a crowd of this size, with sunlight glinting off microphones and camera lenses, all he could do was be prepared to take the bullet meant for Bren.

And he would, in a heartbeat.

By the time they were moving along the halls of Congress, he was sweating. Even then he couldn't relax. Every doorway, every bend in the hallway, offered the perfect opportunity for a gunman. Recent events had proven that all the security in the world couldn't deter a criminal bent on destruction.

When they reached Bren's office he held the

door, his gaze scanning the hallway behind them.

"Good morning." Juana turned from the TV monitor. "I just saw you on the morning news."

Chris planted himself beside her desk. "Ms. Sanchez, I'll need you to screen everyone who enters Bren's offices. If you don't recognize them, they don't come in. Understood?"

She gave him a dazzling smile. "I knew there was a reason why I liked you, Captain." She glanced at Bren. "Did you know the media would be waiting?"

Bren shook her head as she continued toward her inner office.

Behind her Chris muttered, "That was a media ambush, pure and simple."

Juana nodded. "Public officials are considered fair game."

Once inside, out of view of the others, Bren touched a hand to his arm. "There's no sense getting angry."

His eyes narrowed with fury. "Are you serious? Don't get mad? Somebody leaked this to the press. I'd bet everything I own that it was our guy. This is all a game with him. He craves the publicity."

Bren nodded. "I know. And now he has it. There's nothing we can do but make the best of it."

"And hope this guy doesn't try something even more outrageous, just to feed that ego. Or maybe encourage a dozen copycats to crawl out of the woodwork."

Bren pushed her intercom. When Juana's voice came on, Bren asked, "How much time before my first committee meeting?"

"Fifteen minutes."

"Thanks. I'll be ready." Bren sighed as she looked at her appointment schedule. "It would have been nice to have a little time to prepare."

Chris was pacing off his anger. "You would have had the time if it hadn't been for our friendly creep inviting the press to a party."

She walked up beside him and lay a hand on his cheek. "I know you're upset on my behalf—"

"Upset?" He gave an angry huff, then caught himself and closed a hand over hers. She could see him fighting with every breath to bank his temper. "Sorry. That wasn't professional."

"No." She smiled. "It was personal."

"Yeah. It's personal. And that's something new for me."

"Me, too."

He rubbed his lips over hers. "Do you think we have time for...?"

She was already laughing and shaking her head in disbelief. "Men. Didn't you hear? I have colleagues coming here in a few minutes."

"You can't blame a guy for trying." He brushed a kiss over the tip of her nose. "Okay. Get to work, Congresswoman. Until this guy is caught, I'm as much a part of you as your shadow."

For some, familiarity might breed contempt. For Chris it brought respect for the amount of work Bren was able to complete in a single day. Her energy was boundless. Her enthusiasm contagious. She had a way of persuading, cajoling, and occasionally bullying to get her fellow Congressmen in line over her pet issues.

It had never occurred to him that she was involved in so many activities. A presidential commission. An oversight committee on waste and government spending. And, of course, the committee looking into his own police department. Though she was bound to be feeling intimidated by the threat, she hadn't slacked off in her determination to go ahead with the investigation. She had made that clear to the committee today when they'd met in her office.

Now, after sharing lunch together in the congressional dining room, Bren and Chris were walking along the hallway when Chris heard the ringing of his cell phone.

"Banning here."

"Chris." The booming voice of Police Chief Roger Martin had him wincing as he held the receiver away from his ear. "I have some interesting information here. I'd like to share it with you. Could you be in my office within the hour?"

Chris frowned. "As you know, I'm on special assignment."

"I'm well aware of that. But since this is pertinent to your assignment, I think you'll want to look at this."

"I'm on my way." Chris escorted Bren inside her suite of offices, then waited until she'd closed the door to her inner office before saying, "I have to leave you alone. I don't like it, but I'm sure you heard the chief."

She laughed. "Along with half the people walking along the hallway. Is he always that loud?"

Despite his frustration at having to leave her, Chris managed a smile. "He always comes across like a drill sergeant. He can rip an ear off at twenty paces."

"I'm sure it's most effective when he's dressing down an errant officer."

Chris laughed. "The funny thing is, when he's really mad, his voice is so soft you can hardly hear him." He touched a hand to her arm. "I don't know how long this will take, but I'll be back as soon as I can manage. In the meantime..."

"I know." She glanced at the phone ringing on her desk. "I'll be fine."

"Just promise me you'll be careful."

"Promise." She moved to her desk and picked up the phone.

Chris opened her door, then turned for one last word of caution. Seeing Bren already deep in conversation with a colleague, he pointed to his cell phone. Seeing her slight nod, he closed her door.

In the outer office he paused beside Juana's desk. "Keep screening her visitors."

The older woman nodded, then reached for her phone, snatching it up on the second ring.

As Chris walked away he heard her saying, "I'm sorry. Congresswoman Lassiter is tied up on another call at the moment. Would you like to hold, or would you rather she return your call when she's free?"

Free.

He was still frowning as he started along the hallway. Congresswoman Lassiter wouldn't be free until this nutcase was behind bars. Until then, he had an uneasy feeling about leaving her unguarded for even a little while.

Bren stuck her head out of her office and glanced around, seeing that she and Juana were the only ones left.

"Have you heard from Captain Banning?"

Juana shook her head. "Not a word."

"I've tried his cell phone a dozen times." Bren blew out a breath of annoyance. "No answer."

Both women looked up as the door opened. Trevor Sinclair, looking dashing in a crisp, starched uniform, gave one of his dazzling smiles.

"Good evening, Congresswoman."

"Trevor." She nodded toward her assistant. "This is Juana Sanchez. Juana, this is Officer Trevor Sinclair."

"Ms. Sanchez." Leaving the door open, he strolled closer and offered a handshake, before glancing around. "I thought I'd find Chris here."

"He got a call from the chief. But I expected him back long before this."

Trevor arched a brow. "You're alone? Then I guess I'll just stay here until Chris gets back."

"There's no need..." Bren's words trailed off as she caught sight of the hulking form of Noah Swale outside her door.

Seeing the direction of her gaze, Trevor motioned toward her inner office. "Why don't you two go inside? I'll see what Noah wants."

Bren was only too happy to take refuge. Catching Juana's hand, she pulled her along. A few minutes later Trevor returned, looking grim.

"What's wrong?"

"Nothing. I don't want either of you ladies

to worry.'' With an effort he forced himself to smile. ''It's just that Officer Swale couldn't seem to come up with a good reason for being here.'' He went silent for a moment, deep in thought, before saying, ''Look. Why don't I escort both of you to your cars. I'd feel a whole lot better once you're safely locked inside your vehicles.''

Juana glanced at Bren before saying, ''I planned on staying with Congresswoman Lassiter until Captain Banning returned.''

Trevor glanced at his watch. ''Half the building has already emptied. Before long only the night guard will be here.'' He turned to Bren. ''I'd be happy to drive you to wherever you want to go, after we've escorted Ms. Sanchez to her car.''

When Bren hesitated, he added ominously, ''I hate the thought of the two of you alone here, especially with Swale lurking somewhere nearby.''

Bren shivered. ''Chris asked me to wait. I think we should stay here. Would you mind staying with us?''

He shook his head, his smile quick and easy. ''I'll just check in with the chief.'' He turned away and punched in a series of numbers on his cell phone, then said softly, "I'm here with... How soon?" He paused. "Look. I can't just leave the congresswoman and her assistant here alone. Can this wait?" Another pause before he said, "All right. Then I have no choice but to drive the congresswoman home before I head back to the department."

He tucked his cell phone in his pocket and turned with a smile. "The chief agrees that I ought to take you home. Then I'm needed back at the squad room."

Bren and Juana retrieved their belongings from their desks, then followed Trevor from the office. As their heels beat a steady tattoo along the empty hallway, Bren kept turning to glance over her shoulder. She thought she saw a hulking shadow in a doorway. When she looked again it was gone.

By the time they had accompanied Juana to her car, Bren's heart was in her throat.

When Juana drove away Trevor took hold of Bren's arm and walked with her to his waiting police car. Once inside she fastened her seat belt and leaned her head back as the car eased out of the parking slot.

He turned to her. "Where to, Congresswoman?"

"I'm staying at my mother's in Chevy Chase. I'll give you directions as we go."

The day had long ago faded into dusk. A strong wind whipped red and orange leaves into a whirling dance as they sped along the street. Bren could feel her breathing beginning to ease, and realized for the first time just how tense she'd been feeling. She knew Chris would never have left her alone all this time without a good reason.

She turned to Trevor. "I'm really glad you happened along when you did."

"Yeah. Me, too."

She hesitated, then asked, "Is there bad blood between you and Noah Swale?"

"Not that I know of." He gave her a boyish grin. "If you ask me, though, he's just mad at the world. It happens, sometimes, to guys who stay on the streets too long. They see the whole world as the enemy. Look at the way he treated you at our charity dinner."

He turned where she indicated, then followed a street lined with comfortable old houses until she pointed.

"This is where you're staying?"

She nodded.

He turned off the ignition and hurried

around to open her door. As they climbed the steps, she paused at the door to thank him. Just then the door was yanked open, and she looked up. "Pop. I was just about to thank this young officer for driving me home."

Kieran glanced around. "Where's Captain Banning?"

"I don't know. He was called away and never returned. So Trevor offered to step in and bring me here."

"My thanks, young man." Kieran stood aside. "Come in. The least I can do is offer you some dinner."

Bren was already shaking her head. "Trevor has to be back at the station within the hour."

"That's right. But thank you, sir. I appreciate the offer."

He backed away and returned to his car. Before Kieran could close the door, a second pair of headlights turned into the driveway.

Chris watched the retreating police car before slamming out of his car and storming up the steps.

He pushed past Kieran without a word and stalked across the room to where Bren was just discarding her briefcase. "I told you to wait for me. Why the hell would you allow someone else to bring you home?''

She turned to face him. ''You also said you'd be right back. And then I never heard from you. Not one word. I tried your phone a dozen times or more. No answer. When Trevor offered to take me home, I refused. But then I saw Noah Swale sneaking around outside my office.''

''Noah? Are you sure he was sneaking? Maybe he had a valid reason for being there.''

She shook her head in annoyance. ''I've already had a taste of Noah Swale's temper. I decided I didn't want to hang around, waiting for someone who didn't even have the courtesy of phoning me.'' She pinned him with a look that reflected both anger and hurt. ''I trusted you, Chris. And you betrayed that trust. So if you're looking for someone to blame, look in the mirror.''

Before he could say a word in his defense she brushed past him and started up the stairs. Over her shoulder she called, ''Don't hold dinner for me, Pop. I've suddenly lost my appetite.''

Chapter 14

"Hey, big sis." Cameron rapped on Bren's bedroom door. "Pop says you've brooded long enough. Time to get downstairs and join the family."

"I'm not brooding." She yanked open the door and scowled at him. "I never brood."

"Yeah. I can see you're feeling really cheerful." He tugged on a curl. "There's a big family powwow going on. You may want to put in your two cents."

"Sorry. I have plenty of work to occupy my mind. Not interested."

"I think you will be when you hear that

your police captain is insisting on moving us out."

"Moving us..." She swept past him and flounced down the stairs, preparing herself for a knock-down, drag-out argument.

In the great room Chris was talking in low tones to Kieran and Kate. They looked up as she entered.

"What's this about moving us out of our own home?"

Chris decided to ignore the fire in her eyes. "Your security here has been compromised. I spoke with Micah and arranged for all of you to join him and Pru up the street."

"Just like that?" Bren looked from her mother to her grandfather, expecting them to close ranks. "Are you going to tell us what you've learned?"

"I wish I could, Bren, but it isn't public knowledge as yet. What I can tell you is that from the documentation shown me by the chief, your safety and that of your family has been threatened."

"In what way?"

"I can't say. "

"Oh, yes. Of course. It's that precious code of silence, I suppose. And?" she prompted.

"And I intend to set a trap."

"Here in our home?"

He nodded. "That's right. Using one of our detectives as a decoy."

"A decoy?" Bren's eyes narrowed.

When his cell phone rang he snatched it up. "Banning. Good. Right on time."

He crossed to the door and turned the lock, then stood aside as a woman in uniform stepped inside. He quickly closed the door before asking, "Where's your partner?"

"Down the street by now. He dropped me, then took off without lights."

"Good." Chris turned to Bren and her family. "This is Detective Annie McPhail. Annie, this is Congresswoman Lassiter, the one you'll be impersonating."

Bren offered her hand, all the while shaking her head. "You can't be serious. No offense, Detective, but you're about six inches taller than I am, and your hair is long and dark."

The woman pulled a red wig from her pocket. "Don't worry, Congresswoman. In the dark, size can be deceiving."

Kieran looked doubtful. "I agree with Bren. After all, this attacker is someone who has seen Bren before. I'm not certain a red wig is enough to fool him."

Bren turned to Chris. "If you're hoping to catch this man, let me act as decoy."

"Not a chance." Chris refused to look into those pleading eyes, knowing how persuasive she could be. "I've seen too many of these sting operations go wrong. At least with trained police officers we have a chance of avoiding a tragedy."

"Let me at least talk with your chief. I think I could change his mind."

"Be my guest." Chris dialed the number, then handed over his cell phone, all the while knowing what the chief would say. Even someone as persuasive as a congresswoman known for her aggression wouldn't cut through the chief's wall of reserve.

He watched as Bren held the phone a little away from her ear when the chief's voice boomed over the phone. Everyone in the room listened in silence as Bren pleaded her case.

Moments later Chris was relieved to hear the chief's voice shouting, "Do you really think I would allow a member of Congress, the head of the committee investigating my department, to put herself in harm's way? Ms.

Lassiter, you are the reason my people are there, putting their lives on the line. They're doing it to protect you from the person who has been threatening you. I order you and your family to do whatever Captain Banning requests. I trust his judgment completely.''

As Bren handed over the phone to Chris she said, ''I suppose this means that we're all leaving for Micah's house?''

''That's right.'' He turned to Detective McPhail. ''I'll personally escort the Lassiter family down the street. While I'm gone, you can change into civilian clothes and the wig. When I return, we'll put our plan into action.''

She nodded.

Chris herded the family together. At the door he explained, ''No flashlights. We'll use the darkness as a cover. Once you're inside Micah's house, you're free to do as you please, as long as you keep the draperies closed for privacy.''

As they stepped outside he caught Bren's hand and lowered his tone, for her ears alone. ''I hope when this is over you'll give me a chance to explain.''

''Oh, I think I understand already.'' She coolly withdrew her hand from his. ''You have a need to run the show, don't you, Chris?''

He gave a snort of disgust. "Is that what you think? That I'm doing this to prove some sort of point?"

She stopped dead in her tracks. "You left me today, saying you'd be back shortly. I wasn't to leave until I heard from you. Yet you never returned, and you never answered your phone. What was I to do, when I spotted Noah Swale lurking around outside my office? Had it not been for Trevor Sinclair, I'd probably still be cowering in my office. Or is that what you were secretly hoping? That I'd wait for some white knight to come and save me? Sorry. I'm not some timid mouse hiding in a corner, afraid of the big bad cat. I saw an opportunity to leave safely and took it."

When Chris offered no word in his own defense, she followed her family up the steps of Micah's house without a backward glance. But as she stepped inside she caught a glimpse of Chris just before the door was closed and bolted.

There had been in his eyes a bleak look she'd only seen once before. When he'd told her about his sister's death of a drug overdose.

* * *

It had been hours since Bren and her family had settled into Micah's house. They had snacked on pizza from the freezer and gallons of coffee while they discussed this latest bizarre twist in this curious case. Finally the adrenaline had begun to wear off, leaving them exhausted. One by one they'd drifted off. Kieran had taken refuge on a sofa in the den. Cameron was asleep in a recliner in front of the TV. Kate had gone to the upstairs guest room. Micah and Pru were still awake, talking quietly in the master bedroom. It was obvious to everyone that Micah's training in security had him itching to join Chris Banning in the stakeout. But since this was a police operation, he knew better than to offer his assistance. His job now was to remain here with his family, awaiting word that the fly had been caught in their web.

Bren descended to a lower-level apartment that had once been maid's quarters. With a wall of floor-to-ceiling windows and glass doors, it looked out onto a small back garden filled with Pru's beloved perennials. One side of the room was outfitted with Micah's workout equipment, while the other side held a wet bar and sofa bed.

Bren closed the drapes before kicking off her shoes and sitting on the sofa, still nursing the anger that had flared earlier. What right did Chris have to act so all-knowing? After all, he was the one who'd messed up. He was the one who hadn't returned as promised. It was he who hadn't answered his phone or offered any explanation for his strange behavior.

It galled her that everyone in her own family had agreed so readily with Chris and Chief Martin. Without a word of complaint they had moved out of their own home and had been herded like cattle to Micah's. Here she was, about to sleep on a lumpy sofa bed, in the clothes she'd been wearing all day. And what if this didn't turn out as Chris planned? Were they supposed to simply stay here with Micah and Pru for days? Weeks?

She rested her head back against the sofa, closing her eyes. What had she ever seen in Chris Banning? The man was a pompous dictator, out to prove he was right, no matter how much inconvenience he caused others.

Her anger surprised her. It wasn't like her

to be so moody and judgmental. Was this what love did?

Love. The very word annoyed her. Maybe she'd been fooling herself. Maybe, seeing her brothers Micah and Donovan happily married, she'd begun to think there was something missing from her life. Maybe what she'd thought of as love was only her hormones raging.

A soft, rustling sound had her opening her eyes. Was there something outside the window? She got to her feet. But before she could cross the room the draperies seemed to billow inward. There was a muffled tinkling of glass. Without warning a darkened figure slipped inside. As he stepped into the light Bren recognized Trevor Sinclair. In his hand was a gun.

"Trevor. How did you...?" She stared at the high-powered binoculars worn around his neck.

He was grinning. That boyish smile she'd thought so charming. He touched a hand to the binoculars. "They're equipped with night vision. Amazing what you can see. I sat in a ditch yards from your house and watched Detective McPhail. I figure she's the decoy. Right?"

When Bren said nothing, he stepped closer. "Then I witnessed you and your family walking down the street. From the look on your face, I'd say you weren't very happy with Captain Banning." He laughed. "Too bad you had to waste your last moments together in a lovers' spat."

"Last moments?" She couldn't seem to tear her gaze from the gun in his hand.

It was happening again. An armed man, pointing his weapon directly at her, while she was forced to stand there, feeling completely defenseless.

"Yeah. Didn't I tell you? This time I'm not going to make idle threats to scare you. This time I'm going to kill you, Congresswoman. And by the time Captain Banning and Detective McPhail get here, I'll be miles away." He laughed again as he gave her a long, slow look that had her heart thudding. "Think of this as a sort of love game. Everything before was just foreplay. Now we're about to do the dirty deed."

She took a step back. "I don't understand.

What is this about? Why do you want me dead?''

"Because you had to stick your nose where it wasn't wanted. Until you and your committee got the press involved, I had a nice little scam going. While fellow officers looked the other way I've had a free hand in the property room for the past three years. I've helped myself to dozens of guns, which all bring a nice little sum on the black market. But the best thing was the cocaine. I guess I've stolen hundreds of kilos since I found out how lax the security was."

She looked scandalized. "You're a police officer. You took an oath to uphold the law."

"What a joke. Do you realize that the guys on the other side of the law make twice what we make? Why should they get all the profits?"

"There's more than money at stake here. Think about the reputation of your fellow officers. Why would you want to hurt the image of an entire police force?"

"Why?" His smile faded. His eyes narrowed to slits. "I'll tell you why, Congresswoman. I told you my grandfather was a cop years ago."

Bren felt a twinge of guilt. With all that had happened, she'd forgotten to mention Trevor's name to Pop.

The young officer's eyes went flat. "My grandfather needed money to pay my grandmother's medical bills. When he went to his chief for help, he was told there was nothing the police force could do for him. So he decided to take care of it himself. When he came across a shopkeeper who was willing to pay for protection against thugs who'd been breaking into his shop at night, my grandfather realized there were lots more shopkeepers who might pay if they started finding their businesses vandalized. So he started breaking into small shops at night, then, after the shopkeepers were scared enough, he came to them and offered his protection for a fee."

"For a fee? He was an officer of the law. He had no right..."

Bren's words died when he waved the gun in her face.

"What would you know about his rights? He was desperate. Have you ever been desperate?" When she didn't answer he sneered. "Yeah. That's what I thought. You're just like the judge who heard the case. He didn't care about anything except the law. My grandfather was dismissed in disgrace from the force and did time in a federal prison. The men he'd put behind bars made his life a living hell. On his deathbed I gave him my solemn promise that someone would pay."

"Why should someone pay for your grandfather's crime?"

"You know why." The smile was back. Only now Bren realized it was neither boyish nor charming. It was frightening to see the way he could turn it on or off, like an actor striking a pose. "I enjoy the game. That's what this is. A game. It's called what-can-I-do-today-to-make-the-police-force-look-bad-and-get-rid-of-troublemakers-at-the-same-time? And you know what? It's so easy. I always win. People trust me. Like you, Congresswoman. You trusted me more than your own lover-boy. That was such fun. First I disabled his phone. Right there at the station, while he was inside the chief's office. Then I managed to involve him in a…minor fender-bender."

"You caused an accident?" She thought about the fury she'd seen in Chris's eyes. She hadn't bothered to look beyond that, to see his pain. "Was he…hurt?"

"Just enough to rough him up a bit. Lucky for him, he's still walking. But not for much longer. He's getting too close. He's going to have to have a more serious accident. I'll probably have to get rid of the chief, too. He's suspicious. I can see it in his eyes when he looks at me."

"You won't get away with this." Bren wondered how much longer she could remain standing. There was a trembling that had begun in her back and was now spreading down her legs. But she had to keep him talking. It was her only hope. "You've made mistakes, Trevor. Bits and pieces of evidence are being documented. Sooner or later they'll all point to you. And your little game will be over."

"I wouldn't worry about it if I were you, Congresswoman. You won't be around to see how the game ends."

As he took aim, he saw, out of the corner of his eye, the drapes part as Chris stepped through the broken window.

"Too late, Banning." He executed a half turn and fired directly into Chris's chest.

Bren let out a cry as Chris stumbled backward and dropped to his knees, clutching the edge of the drape to keep from falling. No one, she knew, could survive a direct hit to the chest. She couldn't bear to have him die without letting him know how deeply she cared about him. Without a thought to her own safety she raced to his side and dropped to her knees, wrapping her arms around his waist to hold him up. "Oh, Chris. I've been such a fool. Please believe me when I tell you how much I love you."

"How touching. You're breaking my heart." Trevor took aim. "Bye-bye, Congresswoman. You and your lover have made this so much fun."

It was the second time Bren found herself facing death. And once again she met it headon and thought about her father in that split second that the sound of gunfire roared through her brain. She braced herself for the pain of the bullet. When she watched Trevor's knees buckle, and caught sight of the blood spreading across his uniform, she glanced down and saw the gun in Chris's hand.

"Oh, my darling. You're still alive." With a cry Bren watched Chris slide ever so slowly from her arms and collapse on the floor.

She draped herself over his prone body, choking back tears. "Please don't die. Please, Chris. I love you so much. Stay with me."

Moments later, as Detective McPhail raced into the room, she stared at the scene before her.

"He killed him," Bren called, as her family came dashing down the stairs, stopping in their tracks at the sight of so much blood. "Trevor killed Chris. And I couldn't do a thing to stop him."

She felt someone kneel beside her and saw, through her tears, the bulky figure of Noah Swale.

Without a word he unbuttoned Chris's shirt to reveal the full body armor.

"You're going to have one hell of a bruise, pal," he whispered.

"Yeah. I...feel like I have...an elephant on my chest." Chris blinked, then opened his eyes, squinting against the light as he focused on Bren's tear-stained face. "You...all right?"

"Oh, Chris. You're alive. I was so afraid you were..." She couldn't bring herself to speak the word.

"Sorry. Misjudged the son of a—" He

paused for breath, amazed at the amount of pain he was forced to endure. With an effort he lifted a hand to her cheek. "I was so afraid I'd be too late, Bren."

"How did you know he was here?"

Seeing how difficult it was for his friend to speak, Noah explained, "I found his squad car parked directly behind the garden wall. When I reported it, Captain Banning realized we'd played it all wrong. We'd outsmarted ourselves, leaving you alone here and at his mercy."

Chris nodded. "I started running and didn't stop until I got here."

Bren turned to Noah, who was kneeling beside her. "I hope you'll forgive me for all the things I was thinking about you, Officer."

"I deserved them, ma'am. Sorry about the way I mouthed off to you at the charity dinner. Guess I was trying to shoot the messenger. I didn't like what you and your committee were reporting about our police force. I resented any blemish on our fine men and women. But I have to admit, you were right on the money. I realize now that it would have only gotten worse if you hadn't brought it to the public's attention."

"But I allowed my preconceived notions about you to color my judgment. And when I saw you outside my office, I foolishly let Trevor smooth talk me into breaking my word to Chris."

The burly man flushed. "I was outside your office because Chris asked me to keep an eye on you until he could get there."

She nodded toward Chris. "Trevor told me he staged the accident to keep you from reaching me."

"He needed to trick you into revealing where you were staying. He'd already checked out your apartment and mine and knew we weren't there any longer."

"And I led him right here, putting my entire family at risk."

"We're none the worse for wear, lass." Kieran stooped down and gathered her into his arms. She rested there a moment, loving the feel of the old man's arms around her.

When the emergency team arrived with a stretcher, Bren pushed free of her grandfather's arms. "You're not getting away from me, Captain Banning. I'm going to the hospital with you."

"I don't mind. I'm used to dealing with

these things alone.'' He winced as they lifted him.

"You're not alone anymore, Chris." Bren laced her fingers with his as she moved along beside the gurney.

"Indeed you're not, boyo." Kieran walked up to clap a hand on his granddaughter's shoulder.

"You'll never know what that means to me." Chris saluted Kieran and the rest of Bren's family, who stood watching in silence as he and Bren were whisked away, lights flashing, sirens blaring.

Chapter 15

"Time out, boyos." Kieran stepped out onto the back porch and cupped his hands to his mouth to be heard over the shouts of four grown men pushing and shoving. Chris and Cameron had taken on Micah and Donovan in a no-holds-barred, cutthroat game of hoops. "Our Bren's coming on TV now."

The four men grabbed up towels and mopped at sweat as they trooped into the house and settled themselves on the floor of the great room where Kate and her daughters-in-law were already staring at the TV.

Little Taylor pointed as Bren's face was flashed on the screen. "Look. It's Aunt Bren."

Bren stood facing a bank of microphones. "Our committee wishes to commend the Washington, D.C., Police Department for their spirit of cooperation as we investigated corruption within their ranks. They opened their records, made top-secret documents available to us and answered our questions fully and completely. They acknowledged that a single blemish on their reputation has the ability to stain an entire force. They admitted that security was lax in the property division. Guns and drugs were stolen and sold on the street. But, to our great relief, we have discovered that this was no large-scale conspiracy. Rather, it was the work of a single man, who took advantage of the department's code of silence to ply his evil for his own benefit. The officer in question will face criminal prosecution. I have no doubt that he will pay dearly for the choices he made." She set aside her notes and looked directly into the cameras. "Our committee has come away from this investigation with a deep respect for the men and women who daily put their lives on the line for each of us. Greater love hath no man."

As she started to step away, a reporter's voice bellowed over the din. "Congresswoman Lassiter, I understand that as a result of your investigation you found yourself in the line of fire. Can you tell us about it?"

She paused, and those who knew her could see the struggle going on within. But the viewers deserved the truth.

"It is true. The officer in question thought that by killing me he could put a stop to the investigation."

"Does this make you want to give up public life?" the reporter shouted.

Bren smiled. "I came to this job hoping to make a difference. I believe, in some small way, I have. I think for now I'll continue on, doing my best to serve my constituents, and let our fine police officers worry about keeping its citizens safe."

Someone shouted another question, and she shook her head as she turned away from the microphones. "Sorry. I'm late for an appointment."

Bren stepped through the front door of her mother's house and breathed in the wonderful smells of freshly baked bread and dinner cooking. Tossing aside her briefcase, she pushed open the kitchen door and paused to drink in the familiar scene.

Kieran, in his apron, was lifting a huge roasting pan from the oven. Kate was stirring something on the stove. Pru and Andi were showing young Taylor and Cory how to sprinkle grated cheese over sliced vegetables in a shallow baking dish. Donovan was slicing bread still warm from the oven. Micah had just popped the cork on a bottle of champagne, while Cameron, his expensive white shirt splattered with gravy, was extolling the virtues of his latest female conquest.

And there, in the midst of the activity, was Chris, the sleeves of his uniform rolled to his elbows as he prepared his own salad dressing. He and Kieran were laughing as they shared a private joke about police work.

"Bren." Kate was the first to spot her daughter standing there.

"Hey, little sis." Micah handed her a tulip glass of champagne. "That was quite a dog-and-pony show."

She grinned. "Thanks."

"It would have been a lot better," Cameron said as he brushed a kiss over her cheek, "if you'd have mentioned your family by name once or twice.''

''That would have added another hour to her press conference.'' Donovan dropped a hand on her shoulder. ''You did good.''

''High praise, coming from you.''

''Yeah. Well, I may not tell you often enough, but I think you're pretty terrific.''

Kieran crossed the room and gave her a fierce hug. ''I was proud of you, Mary Brendan. Standing up there, saying such fine things about the police.''

''They came from the heart, Pop.''

''I know.'' He kissed her cheek before returning to the stove.

Kate studied Bren, seeing the way she kept glancing toward Chris, who hadn't said a word. Dropping an arm around her daughter's waist, she said, ''Let's go in the other room.''

When they were alone in the great room, Kate caught her daughter's hands in hers. ''What's wrong?''

''Just tired, I guess.''

Kate shook her head before squeezing Bren's hands. ''I know you too well, darling. You were never very good at lying. What's bothering you?''

"It's seeing Chris here with the family."

Kate arched a brow. "I should think that would please you. It means that we've all accepted him as one of us."

Bren swallowed, knowing she couldn't hide the truth from her mother. Besides, she needed to unburden her heart. "I think it's grand that the family loves him. I'm just not sure if he's here because of me, or because he's discovered how much he loves being part of a large family. Let's face it. He has more in common with Pop or Micah or Donovan than he does with me."

"Is that what you think?" Suddenly a slow smile curved Kate's lips. Squeezing her daughter's hands she said, "I think it's best if Chris speaks for himself." With a quick kiss on her daughter's cheek, she hurried away.

When Bren turned, Chris was standing directly behind her.

She flushed. "You had no right to sneak up on me like that."

"It's one way to get to the heart of the problem." He frowned. "For such a smart woman, you can come up with some…weird assumptions."

"Weird?" She brought her hand to her hips. "I'll have you know…"

"It takes two to fight, Mary Brendan. And right now, you're the only one in the mood for it." He touched a finger to her lips to silence her protest. "In case you haven't noticed, we've been racing on a treadmill for an awfully long time now. You're involved in your congressional duties, while I've been wrapping up this investigation. And when you're not meeting with some committee, I'm pulling double duty until we replace Trevor. On top of that you're going off to your apartment late at night while I race off to mine whenever there's time. And then there are your family commitments."

"What are you saying? That we should both cool it for a while?"

He smiled. "There you go again. Jumping to conclusions. I'm just saying that there hasn't been any time for us to talk about our feelings. Maybe we ought to do that right now."

She lifted her chin, anticipating a blow to the heart. "I suppose you want to go first."

"Yeah. I do." He took her hand between both of his, studying the way it looked. "To those who don't know you, you come across as so small and fragile.''

At her arch expression he merely smiled. ''But I've learned that looks can be deceiving. There's nothing fragile about you, Mary Brendan Lassiter. You've got the heart of a warrior.''

The smoldering look he gave her had her throat going dry.

''That's what first hooked me. But that was just the beginning. There are so many layers to you, I feel as though it'll take me a lifetime or two to get to know everything about you.'' He drew her closer and touched a hand to her cheek. ''Now that I've met you, Bren, I can't imagine my life without you. But I'm not talking about moving in together. Though I want that, I want more. I want it all. The vows, the lifelong commitment. I want you to marry me, Bren.''

''About time.'' It was Cory's voice that had them looking up as the entire family came rushing into the room, shouting and screaming.

Bren's smile turned to a scowl. ''How could you let them do this, Mom?''

Kate was laughing too hard to stop. "You know how we love to eavesdrop."

Pru and Andi were nodding and giggling.

"I'm sorry, Bren," Pru said between laughs. "But it looks like it's rubbed off on us, as well. Andi and I have become experts at eavesdropping the Lassiter way. Haven't we, Andi?"

Her sister-in-law was laughing so hard all she could do was nod her head.

"Okay, big sis." Cameron lounged in the doorway. "Give the guy an answer so we can get on with dinner."

"Oh, you'd like that, wouldn't you?" She scowled at him, then turned to include the rest of her family. "Sorry. You'll just have to wait. I'm going to find some privacy in this madhouse, if it kills me."

Bren grabbed Chris by the hand and led him out the door and onto the front porch. Just as she lifted herself on tiptoe to wrap her arms around his neck, a car turned into the driveway and Noah Swale and the chief stepped out and sprinted up the steps.

"Well, well. Just the two we're looking for." Chief Martin was beaming. "The entire force was cheering at the end of your press conference, Congresswoman.''

"I'm glad." She glanced over at Noah Swale, who was grinning from ear to ear.

He wiped sweat from his forehead. "Did we catch you two at a bad time?"

"You might say that. Excuse me." Desperate for privacy, Bren caught Chris by the hand and led him around to the backyard. She paused beneath the basketball hoop. "Ah. Alone at last."

"We'd better be." Chris drew her into his arms. "Because if I don't get your answer soon, I'm going to toss you over my shoulder and carry you off to the nearest justice of the peace."

"There's not a chance of that happening. Not in the Lassiter family. If you want to marry me, you'll have to face the fact that we like our weddings like everything else in our lives—larger than life."

"Is that a yes?"

She shrugged. "I suppose, now that I've found my perfect match…"

He grinned. "You think I'm perfect?"

She arched a brow. "Who says I'm talking about you?"

He dragged her close and brushed his mouth over hers, sending her heart into overdrive. "Give me his name and I'll break him in half."

She couldn't help laughing. "His name is Chris Banning."

"Hmm." He closed his eyes. "I've heard of him. A great guy. In fact, the finest man I've ever known. I've also heard he's madly in love with a woman with the crazy name of Mary Brendan Lassiter."

"Hmm. Maybe she can't decide if she's a man or a woman."

"She's all woman." He framed her face with his hands. "And I hope she'll be mine." His tone turned serious. "Bren, I know it won't be easy with two busy careers. But I happen to believe we can make it work. That is, if you love me as much as I love you."

"I do, Chris. I love you so much I can hardly bear it when we're not together."

"I can remedy that."

As they came together in a blazing kiss, they heard the sound of cheering. This time when they looked up, they could see that Chief Martin and Noah Swale had joined the family around the big bay window in the kitchen.

The back door opened and the family came streaming out to congratulate the happy couple. Bren found herself being hugged by her brothers and their wives, who seemed absolutely delighted at the prospect of another family wedding.

Kieran gathered his granddaughter into his arms and hugged her fiercely. "I'm so happy for you, lass."

Until that moment Bren had been completely composed. But when she felt the dampness of his tears, it started tears of her own, until she and her grandfather were laughing and weeping together.

At last they drew apart, and Kieran turned to Chris to offer a handshake. "It's pleased I am, Captain Christopher Banning, that you'll be joining our family. You'll make a fine, proud addition to it."

"No more pleased than I am, Pop."

Bren wondered if Chris realized what he'd just said. He hadn't even called his own adopted father by the title. And yet here he was, letting the name roll off his tongue as though he'd been saying it for a lifetime.

She dropped an arm around her mother,

who was watching through a mist of tears.
"Are you happy for us, Mom?"

"Oh, I am, darling. But I was just thinking
that it's a bittersweet moment. You're my only
daughter."

Bren nodded. "You're not losing a daughter, Mom, you're gaining a—"

"A man in uniform," Kate added softly. "It
will be nice having that in our home once
more. If your father were here, I know he
would approve."

Bren smiled gently. "He does, Mom."

Kate sighed, and mother and daughter
shared a quiet moment.

When Chris turned and gathered her into his
arms, the clouds suddenly parted and the evening sun sent out soft rays like a benediction.
Though there wasn't even a hint of a breeze,
a shower of golden leaves drifted to the
ground.

As she and Chris came together in a joyous
kiss, Bren heard her father's voice, like a sigh
of the wind. Just a whisper. But she knew,
without a doubt, that Riordan Lassiter was still
there with them, sharing their joy, just as he
had shared their sorrow.

"Welcome home," she whispered against Chris Banning's lips.

"Home." Chris could hardly contain the happiness he felt at this moment. For a man who had once had no home, this was heaven. And this woman was his guardian angel.

"I intend to spend the rest of my life deserving you, Congresswoman."

"I'll hold you to that, Captain Banning."

"Now," he whispered against her ear, "as much as I love your family, do you think we could slip away to a more…intimate place?"

Bren was grinning as she caught his hand. "Don't hold dinner, Pop."

Laughing like two conspirators, they made a dash to his car. Once inside he dragged her into his arms and kissed her until they were both breathless.

Against her lips he muttered, "Do you think there's anybody hanging around your office today?"

"Not a chance. But I'm not sure what you have in mind is appropriate in the halls of Congress."

"It's probably not legal, either." He kissed her again before turning the key in the ignition.

As they backed out of the driveway they caught sight of her family standing together in the open doorway.

Bren blew them a kiss before turning to Chris with a look of love. She couldn't wait to spend the rest of her life with this man who owned her heart so completely.

*   *   *   *   *

Be sure to look for Cameron's story,
the final book in
THE LASSITER LAW *series,*
coming in May 2002,
only from
Silhouette Intimate Moments.

Silhouette®

INTIMATE MOMENTS™

presents:

Romancing the Crown

*With the help of their powerful allies,
the royal family of Montebello is
determined to find their missing heir.
But the search for the beloved prince
is not without danger—or passion!*

**Available in April 2002:
SECRET-AGENT SHEIK
by Linda Winstead Jones (IM #1142)**

Under deep cover, Sheik Hassan Kamal headed to Texas hoping to
discover the secrets of a suspected terrorist. But he never expected to
fall for Elena Rahman, his archenemy's beautiful daughter....

*This exciting series continues throughout
the year with these fabulous titles:*

*Available only from Silhouette Intimate Moments
at your favorite retail outlet.*

Silhouette®

Where love comes alive™

Visit Silhouette at www.eHarlequin.com

SIMRC4

This Mother's Day Give Your Mom A Royal Treat

Win a fabulous one-week vacation in Puerto Rico for you and your mother at the luxurious Inter-Continental San Juan Resort & Casino. The prize includes round trip airfare for two, breakfast daily and a mother and daughter day of beauty at the beachfront hotel's spa.

INTER·CONTINENTAL
San Juan
RESORT & CASINO

Here's all you have to do:

Tell us in 100 words or less how your mother helped with the romance in your life. It may be a story about your engagement, wedding or those boyfriends when you were a teenager or any other romantic advice from your mother. The entry will be judged based on its originality, emotionally compelling nature and sincerity.
See official rules on following page.

Send your entry to:
Mother's Day Contest

In Canada	**In U.S.A.**
P.O. Box 637	P.O. Box 9076
Fort Erie, Ontario	3010 Walden Ave.
L2A 5X3	Buffalo, NY
	14269-9076

Or enter online at www.eHarlequin.com

PRROY

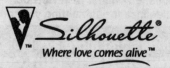